FETLOCKS HALL

The Enchanted Pony

Babette Cole

BLOOMSBURY

LONDON BERLIN NEW YORK SYDNEY

Bloomsbury Publishing, London, Berlin, New York and Sydney

First published in Great Britain in June 2011 by Bloomsbury Publishing Plc
36 Soho Square, London, W1D 3QY

A CIP catalogue record of this book is available from the British Library

ISBN 978 0 7475 9934 0

MIX
Paper from
responsible sources
FSC
www.fsc.org
FSC® C018072

Typeset by Hewer Text UK Ltd, Edinburgh
Printed in Great Britain by Clays Ltd, St Ives Plc, Bungay, Suffolk

1 3 5 7 9 10 8 6 4 2

www.bloomsbury.com

www.babette-cole.com

To Sophie

Rogues Gallery

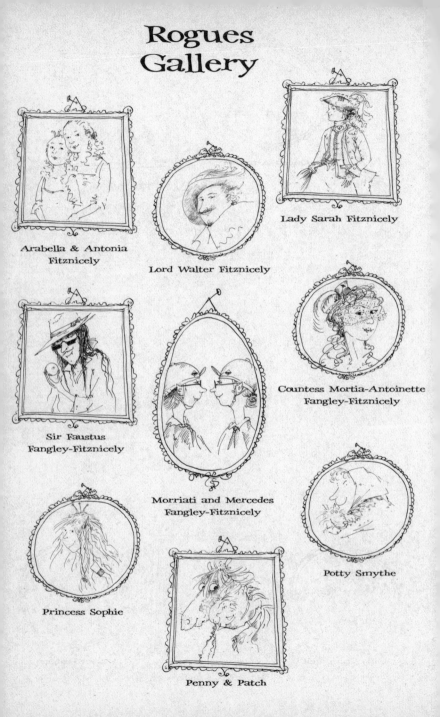

Arabella & Antonia
Fitznicely

Lord Walter Fitznicely

Lady Sarah Fitznicely

Sir Faustus
Fangley-Fitznicely

Morriati and Mercedes
Fangley-Fitznicely

Countess Mortia-Antoinette
Fangley-Fitznicely

Princess Sophie

Penny & Patch

Potty Smythe

Queen Amazon

King Rufus

Henrietta
Wellington-Green

Ben Faloon

Matt Khareef

Bunty Bevan

Peter Fixcannon

Carlos Cavello

Gilly Jumpwell

Philippa
Horsington-Charmers

Sam Hedges

CHAPTER ONE

A Mixed Blessing

'Parents,' sighed Portia Manning-Smythe, head-mistress of Fetlocks Hall Pony School, 'can be a mixed blessing!'

She had just finished a telephone call from Mr and Mrs Simms about their daughter, Penny. They were concerned that her letters and emails home seemed to be full of ponies and nothing to do with any school work. Potty Smythe had reassured them that Penny was doing extremely well at her lessons

1

and that she had probably thought school work was very matter-of-fact and not necessary to mention in her letters. Ponies, on the other hand, are much more exciting to a ten-year-old pony-mad little girl, so naturally she'd want to tell her parents all about her adventures with them.

Mr and Mrs Simms had *no* idea what sort of adventures Penny was having at this very unusual pony school, where extraordinary things happen. In fact, Penny was not only an exceptionally talented horsewoman, but just happened to be the hundredth Unicorn Princess of Equitopia, the Kingdom of the Unicorns. She possessed magical pony powers and was a very important child indeed! She'd ONLY saved Equitopia and Terrestequinus (our planet) from invasion by the wicked Devlipeds. If those nasty, fire-breathing, scaly little red ponies had gained control of these two worlds they would have made life extremely unpleasant for all of us!

Fetlocks Hall had a very important role to play in Equitopia. Its main task was to find and educate very special equichildren who might one day become A students at the school. On reaching this level, pupils can receive magical powers similar to Penny's. While the unicorns are responsible for keeping the mythical scales called the Equilibrium of Goodness balanced in favour of good, the wicked Devlipeds are always plotting to steal them. Their plan is to tip the balance towards evil so that they can make the two worlds as nasty as their own. A students have the power to assist the reigning Unicorn Princess to protect the scales, and therefore keep Equitopia and Terrestequinus safe.

This, of course, was S.U.S. (Secret Unicorn Society) business and that was highly secret. Parents, unless they themselves were past Fetlocks A students, could never be told about the other-worldly side of Fetlocks Hall.

Potty Smythe smiled to herself and took a gulp of tea from her favourite tin mug.

'... And her parents want to know how Penny's doing at computer studies!' she giggled.

It had been predicted by Valentine Silverwings, King of the Unicorns, that Penny would come to Fetlocks Hall. He had given her certain magical gifts which she had earned at her coronation by passing some very rigorous and scary tests. The Lance of Courage protected her against all evil, the Vial of Unicorn Tears helped her to heal all wounds and illnesses, and Queen Starlight's Horn, with its magical music, tamed any wild beast or monster. There was no way Penny or Potty Smythe could share this information with *ordinary* mortals because it was S.U.S. business, but they could tell their extraordinary friends, the Fitznicely family – Lady Sarah, Sir Walter and their mischievous twin daughters, Arabella and Antonia, who were the resident ghosts at Fetlocks Hall. They were all former unicorn royalty and they helped Penny rule as current Unicorn Princess.

Her *everyday* life was supported by her fab chums and teammates, The Fetlocks Hall Flyers, Sam, Pip, Dom, Carlos and Matt. Recently two new pupils had joined the crew. Morri and Merc were the Veggipire children of Lady Mortia-Antoinette and Sir Faustus Fangley-Fitznicely, the unusual inhabitants from the Dower House in the woods near Fetlocks Hall. They were actually hundreds of years old but being Veggipires they could be whatever age they wanted. They'd chosen to be twelve and thirteen years old. *They* knew Penny was a Unicorn Princess but kept the Equitopian secret safe as Penny did theirs. The other children and their parents had no idea that the Fangley-Fitznicelys could turn into bats whenever they liked!

Potty Smythe sighed as she sorted through a huge pile of letters on her desk from pupils' mothers and fathers who, like Penny's, seemed to be feeling left out of their children's school life.

Mr and Mrs Goodfellow had written to say they were worried about their daughter Stephanie, who had asked if she could stay at Fetlocks during the school holidays instead of coming home at all!

Tumbleweed, the little Exmoor pony belonging to Susie Hamilton's parents, hated leaving the school at the end of term so much he refused to go into his trailer. Even Penny, who had the magical gift of Equalese, enabling her to talk to ponies, could not persuade him.

The Waterford family from Ireland were concerned that their son's pony, Coolin, was not jumping as well as expected. Potty Smythe knew how she could solve that problem. She'd get Penny to jump him for Seamus because one of the special gifts King Valentine had given her was the art of Equibatics. She could actually fly ponies, so jumping was no problem.

Herr Klimt, one of the most ambitious parents, was moaning because his daughter's pony was not getting good enough marks in his freestyle dressage to music. Penny, however, had already spoken to the little German pony and discovered that he hated the music and found it too difficult to change legs to the beat. Penny possessed the gift of Equiballet and could make ponies dance. She and Rheingold worked out a new routine to different music. The result was that Potty Smythe received another letter a few weeks later from Herr Klimt, enclosing a cheque to pay for a much-needed new dressage arena.

Although parents were very important as they paid fees to keep the school going, Potty Smythe also wanted to keep relatives happy and informed of their children's school progress. This was all very well but there were other important things for her to do at Fetlocks Hall, like keeping out Devlipeds, finding enough money to run the place and stopping the authorities closing it down! But school fees and new parents were always needed, so something extra had to be done to keep the present parents happy and attract others with the kind of children Fetlocks needed. She decided to hold a staff meeting to see if any of the teachers could come up with a clever idea as to how this could be done.

They all met up next Monday morning in H.Q. (the headmistress's study).

'What about an emailed newsletter at the end of each term?' said Quentin Theary from Physics.

'Or a parent–teacher association with monthly meetings?' suggested Miss Mappit, the geography teacher.

These and similar suggestions seemed good ideas

but Potty Smythe was looking for something more spectacular that could attract new parents as well.

The teachers were all sitting round scratching their heads when Potty's two deerhounds ran over to the balcony window and wagged their tails. They had noticed Penny flying her best pony friend, Patch, around the park. Of course no one else could see this as Penny was invisible when Equibatic to anyone except Potty, the Fitznicely family, ponies, dogs, unicorns and Devlipeds.

'I bet I know someone who could come up with the answer,' thought Potty Smythe, reversing towards the window and giving Penny the secret 'both thumbs up' sign behind her back, indicating that she needed to talk to her.

On her second lap of the great house Penny noticed the signal and landed Patch at the front of the Hall. She slipped off his brown and white back, gave him a pat and raced up the stone steps to the main entrance. Her magical gifts were hidden under the third step and guarded by two stone unicorns on either side. As she dashed past they saluted her with the usual rainbow of stars from their eyes.

'Thanks, Hippolita and Rain,' said Penny in Equalese.

Moments later Penny knocked on the door of H.Q. Potty Smythe opened it and invited her inside.

'Ah, Penny,' she said with a wink and a smile, 'come to fetch those new pony magazines for the library, have you? There they are, on my desk.'

'Of course, Miss,' said Penny with a smile, picking up the bundle. 'Will there be anything else I can do?'

'Well,' continued the headmistress, 'we were all trying to think of a way of getting parents involved in the school a little more. As a Fetlocks student, what do you think your own people would like?'

'That's easy,' said Penny. 'How about a parents' day where we can all show off what we have learned – and the ponies, of course. Something like a county show or country fair.'

'Excellent idea!' cried the headmistress, turning to her astonished staff, who were staring over their tea-cups. Everyone agreed it was a brilliant thought.

'Thank you, Penny,' grinned Potty Smythe. 'Now run along with those . . . and by the way, Patch is eating the petunias.'

CHAPTER TWO

The Phantom
in the Woods

Penny told the rest of The Flyers about the parents' day plan while they were washing grooming kit brushes later that morning.

'We could do a real Fetlocks Hall Horse Show,' she said.

'With demos for the parents on pony club games, eventing, showjumping, dressage, polo – everything we've learned here!' added Sam Hedges. She did not have any parents as they had been killed in a hunting accident, but she was always keen to show off her wonderful horsemanship at shows and events.

'We will have to include some other skills besides our pony ones,' said Ethelene Giggabit (Gig to her friends). A real little computer geek and honorary member of The Flyers, Gig had already thought of making a website for the show and producing a DVD of the day for all the parents to take home.

'When do you think Potty Smythe is planning this parents' day?' said Carlos. 'I would love my father to see our polo team. He is coming over to represent Brazil for the Nations Cup showjumping competition at the Royal International Horse Show soon. It would be great if he could bring his puissance horse, Negra, with him because I could give a high-jump demonstration on her.'

'As long as you don't enter her for the "Chase Me Charlie",' said Dom. 'Our ponies would never be able to follow *her* over a jump and leave it standing. No way could they jump as high as Negra. Doesn't she hold the world record? My folks would be pleased to come up from Cornwall to watch that.'

'Merc and I could do some acting on our ponies to music,' said Morri Fangley-Fitznicely.

'What a great idea!' grinned his sister, showing her strange sharp little teeth. 'We could do something really thrilling to music on Moonwalk and Nightsafe. Mama and Papa can provide the props.'

The other children loved the idea as much as they liked Merc and Morri, even though they did have some rather strange ways. They looked pretty weird with their pale skin, black hair, dark sunglasses and matching black ponies, but were really competitive and full of fun.

'My parents are bringing my Arabian horse, Shaab, over from Dubai for me,' said Matt shyly. 'I have taught him some tricks. He is very intelligent. I could dress as a Bedouin horseman and put on a good show of sabre work.'

Pip dropped her brushes and ran into the tack room.

'What's up with her?' said Matt. 'Did I say something wrong?'

'No,' said Dom. 'What's wrong is that Pip is upset hearing us talk about our parents like this. Hers went missing two years ago and no one has any idea what happened to them. They were equine vets working with zebras in Africa. They just completely vanished out there!'

He put down his brushes and followed her into

the tack room, where poor Pip sat weeping. He put his arm around her and she cried floods of tears on his shoulder. Penny and the other children crept in and gave her a big Fetlocks Hall Flyers hug.

'I'd give anything to see my mummy and daddy again,' she sniffed.

'And I'd do anything to find them,' thought Penny. If only she could somehow use her magical pony powers to find Mr and Mrs Horsington-Charmers she could make Pip's wish come true.

'Let's all go for a nice ride in Middlemarsh Wood,' said Sam, knowing it would cheer Pip up to get out on her lovely pony Waggit. 'Someone's put some jumps up in there and I'm dying to try them out.'

The someone was actually Henrietta Wellington-Green, head girl at Fetlocks. Peter Fixcannon, the handsome school vet, had decided to build some jumps out of fallen branches and logs in the wood for the children as a surprise. Henry had the most awful crush on the vet, so was delighted to help him at any time.

School work was finished for the day and there was plenty of time before the ponies' teatime to go for a ride.

They followed Sam on her brave pony, Landsman, along the rides until she found the line of jumps.

'Come on, you lot,' she yelled over her shoulder. The others all screamed a good view holla and shot after her over the fences at a mad gallop.

They pulled up giggling and laughing and made their way through a leafy glade in the centre of the wood. Carlos's pony, Budget, suddenly stopped and blew down her nostrils.

'Come on, girl, what have you seen?' said Carlos, patting her neck. She was frozen to the spot as if she had seen a ghost.

'What is it, Budget?' said Penny in Equalese. Of course, no one else could hear this question as pony language can only be heard and spoken by Unicorn Royalty.

'I just saw a funny-looking palomino pony over there behind that big elm tree,' said Budget. 'It had the body of a pony but from its shoulders up it was a little girl!'

'Oh, come on, Mum,' said her daughter Shilling, whom Dom was riding. 'That's impossible. I know you are twenty-four and going a bit senile . . . but honestly!'

Budget gave her daughter a nip and told her not to be so cheeky.

The children and their ponies continued along the path on their way back to the Hall. Penny was curious about what Budget had said. She was a wise old pony and certainly not senile. She was very observant and never made mistakes. Penny was determined to find out more about this apparition.

After evening stables at 6 p.m., Penny tacked up Patch again and set off for Middlemarsh Wood. The sun was low in the sky, making dark shadows among the trees. Patch padded softly along the rides until they reached the clearing with the big elm tree where Budget had seen the phantom pony.

Penny decided they should stay here for a bit and see if anything happened. She dismounted and sat under the tree. Patch quietly nibbled the grass by her side. After a little while he looked up and snorted just like Budget had done earlier. Penny could hear someone crying softly. At first she thought it might be Pip, who had probably come out again on Waggit to be alone with her thoughts of lost parents, but she was wrong.

Very quietly, she and Patch moved towards the sobbing sound. There in the shadows, half hidden by a hawthorn bush, was a palomino pony. Startled, it leapt forward and turned to face her. Penny could not believe what she was seeing. Exactly as Budget had described, there was a pony with no neck whatsoever where it should have been. Instead it had the torso, arms, neck and head of a girl with very long blonde hair similar to Penny's. In fact, she looked very like Penny except for her pony body and rather pointed ears.

Patch's mouth fell open. 'Good heavens! What is that?' he said.

Penny walked over to the little girl/pony and offered her a tissue from her pocket to dry her tears.

'Who are you?' she said in Equalese.

'I am an ugly Centaureen, that's who I am!' cried the creature. 'I am half horse and half human – neither one thing nor the other. I'm just a mess!'

'What's your name?' asked Penny.

'If I told you my real name in my own language it would probably pierce your ears, so you can call me Sophie.'

'Pleased to meet you, Sophie,' said Penny, holding out her hand. 'I'm Penny Simms.'

'And the hundredth Unicorn Princess,' continued Sophie, shaking Penny's hand. 'Oh, I know who you are. You see, Equitopia is not just full of unicorns. There are many enchanted ponies there, Centaurs included. I have left that world and come to yours

15

because I want to go to school like other children. I want to go to Fetlocks Hall.'

Penny could see there might be a problem with that straight away.

'Sophie,' she said kindly, 'are Centaurs able to make themselves seen to ordinary humans?'

'Oh yes, I can if I like,' said Sophie, 'and that's exactly what I intend to do. Oh please, Princess Penny, please, please take me to Aunt Portia and get me enrolled right away!'

'But, Sophie,' cried Penny, 'it's impossible! Present-day humans will never have seen someone like you before. You would become a curiosity and your life would be miserable. They may even put you in a museum or a zoo!'

Sophie let out an ear-piercing wail. Penny covered her ears but poor Patch could not. He reared up and shot out of the wood as fast as his short legs could carry him. Sophie started crying again.

'Now look what I have done,' she sobbed. 'Your pony will have earache for a week or even be permanently deaf because of me. I am hopeless!'

Penny was concerned for Patch.

'I can mend him,' she said, 'but I have to get back to Fetlocks to pick up the cure.'

'Oh yes, you will have Unicorn Tears for that,' said

Sophie, 'and you can fly ponies. If you can fly me, hop up on my back and let's go.'

Penny vaulted on to Sophie's back and held on to her waist. '*Let's Fly!*' she commanded and Sophie rose into the air.

'I've never done this before, by the way,' said the Centaureen as they flew out of the wood towards the school. 'It's really quite fun!'

'Sophie,' said Penny, 'you have to promise me you will not make yourself visible when we land in case anyone is around. I promise to find a way of teaching you school work privately myself. If people can see you my cover will be blown and the S.U.S. secrets will be out!'

Sophie agreed. As an Equitopian she was bound after all to keep that world a secret.

Penny and Sophie landed at the front steps to Fetlocks Hall. Penny ran up to the third one and it sprang open, revealing her three magical gifts lying on their golden cushion. The vial of Unicorn Tears spun into her hand. Then she leapt on to Sophie's back and they flew off in search of Patch.

They found the little pony standing in his stable with his head down. His poor ears were hurting terribly and he was shaking with fear because now he was completely deaf. Penny trickled a tiny drop of

Unicorn Tears into each ear. Patch was cured instantly. He breathed a sigh of relief and rubbed his head on Penny's shoulder. Sophie was really sorry for what she had done and promised to have more self-control in future. She wondered if the Unicorn Tears could transform her body.

'They only work on something that is ill or wounded,' said Penny. 'You are in perfect health for a Centaureen and in fact you are very beautiful.'

Sophie thanked her new friend for her kind words but still refused to believe she was anything but ugly.

'When will you start teaching me?' she asked.

'I'll meet you by the elm tree tomorrow night after homework,' said Penny. 'We'd better start with the alphabet and how to write the letters from A to Z.'

Sophie clapped her hands and would have squealed with delight but Penny quickly put her hand over her mouth in case she deafened any more ponies.

They said goodnight to Patch and walked over to the park gate leading to the wood.

'I never thought I'd have a real human friend like you, Penny,' said Sophie.

'Well, I've never had a real Centaureen for one either,' laughed Penny.

They gave each other a hug. Sophie waved farewell, kicked up her heels and galloped away across the park into the night.

CHAPTER THREE

A Lesson Well Learned

Penny made her way back to the main house. She twisted the wooden unicorn at the bottom of the flight of stairs as this was the secret signal for summoning her ghostly friends, the Fitznicely family.

Arabella and Antonia were already out of their portraits, where they rested when not haunting the place. They were tearing along the top of the upper banisters. They had taken their heads off and were chucking them to each other like balls. Arabella missed Antonia's head and it bumped down the stairs and landed at Penny's feet.

'Good evening, dear sister Penny,' said Antonia's head.

'You really must stop doing this,' said Penny, picking it up with both hands. 'It makes me feel quite sick!'

Antonia's head grinned at Penny as she handed it back to the little ghost's headless body accompanying her sister down the stairs.

'Do you know Potty Smythe is planning a parents' day at the school?' asked Penny.

'Yes,' said Antonia, screwing her head back on. 'We ghosts are not going to be left out so we are going to have one as well. Everyone's coming, including our cousins the de Parrotts and the Montecutes. I suppose we'll have to invite that old carbuncle Count Blackdrax too.'

'I will have to send to Paris for a new gown, dear,' said Lady Sarah Fitznicely to her husband, Sir Walter, as they floated down from their portraits. 'I cannot show up at the parents' day in anything but the best. You can be sure my dear sister-in-law, Countess

Mortia-Antoinette, will look stunning as always and we can't let our side of the family down.'

'Of course. You shall have only the best, my love,' said Sir Walter. 'Hang the expense! Ah, there you are, Penny. And what have you been up to today?'

Penny told the Fitznicelys about her new friend Sophie. Arabella and Antonia could not wait to meet her. During their reign as twin Unicorn Princesses they had never met a Centaureen but they did know about them.

'They are actually very warlike mythequines,' said Arabella. 'They are great archers and sword-fighters. It is possible for them to make themselves visible to ordinary mortals but they have not done so since ancient Greek times.'

'I believe their tribe is called the Kentauroi,' added Arabella. 'The female members were called Kentaurides or Centaurides. I suppose a little girl of that kind would be known as a Centaureen. They are very rare. It is supposed to be lucky to see one.'

Sir Walter and Lady Sarah looked worried. Penny assured them her secret and those of Equitopia were safe, because Sophie had promised not to make herself visible to ordinary humans in return for Penny teaching her.

'They are quite determined,' said Sir Walter. 'It's going to be impossible to keep her out of the school entirely, but as long as she remains as invisible as us, I see no harm in it.'

Penny soon found out that Sir Walter was right about Sophie.

The next evening after homework Penny flew Patch over to Middlemarsh Wood, with her satchel slung over her back crammed with early learning books, a jotter and pens. Sophie was eagerly waiting for them to land in the clearing. Penny thought Patch might be helpful during the lessons because he was a pony and Sophie was almost one. Penny was not sure whether a Centaureen thought more like a horse than a human or the other way round.

Sophie curled up her pony legs and sat down next to Penny and Patch. Penny showed her how to hold a pen and make marks in the jotter. To her surprise Sophie took to this right away and started to draw the most amazing detailed illustrations about her life as a Centaureen. She soon filled up the whole jotter with drawings of Equitopian life and the other mythequines there. Penny was intrigued with the drawings of enchanted ponies as she had never seen anything like them before.

Penny tried to teach her the alphabet, but it seemed Sophie had one of her own.

'A is for apple,' said Penny, pointing to an alphabet book with a large picture of an apple.

'No, it's not,' said Sophie, drawing an arrow through the apple. 'It's for archery!'

'OK,' said Penny. 'That will do just as well. B is for bee.'

'B is for berrymunder,' said Sophie.

'What's that?' asked Patch.

Sophie drew a strange lumpy-looking fruit. 'They are delicious!' she said.

'C,' said Penny, 'must be for Centaur and not cat, then?'

'Right!' said Sophie. 'D is for Devliped. I know you've met a few of those nasty things, and E is for Epona, the goddess who protects all horses and their keepers.'

Penny was fascinated by Sophie's unusual way of looking at things. She turned letters into pictures. 'I' was drawn as something she called an 'impaler', a kind of dagger. 'J' was turned into a drawing of a 'juta', her word for the quiver holding her arrows. 'K' was not for kite but for a strange wild-looking horse with fins for feet known as a Kelpie.

Penny and Patch had never heard of them.

'They are very tricky customers,' said Sophie. 'They always live by water and they are shape-shifters that can disguise themselves in any form they like. Once a child is selected, they can steal their parents and freeze them in time. The spell can last for up to two years until they decide to pounce on that child. They often appear as their parents or some other form connected with them. The naughty things encourage the child on to their sticky backs, from which it is hard to dismount. Once a child is stuck on, they plunge under the water, drown them and eat them.'

'How awful!' said Patch. 'I hope they never steal any of our Fetlocks children or their parents.'

A cold shiver went down Penny's spine. She remembered that Pip's parents had been mysteriously missing for two years.

'Maybe they already have!' she said. 'Perhaps that's what happened to Pip's mother and father! Can the spell ever be broken, Sophie?'

The little Centaureen pricked her pony ears and turned to Penny.

'Only by a true Unicorn Princess,' she said.

Penny explained about Pip's lost parents and how she wanted to find them. Sophie said their disappearance did indeed sound like the work of a Kelpie and that she would help in any way she could. It would mean a trip to Equitopia to find the Kelpies' sinister hideout, where they stored their time-frozen prey, but first Sophie wanted to have her school lessons.

She appeared to learn very quickly, although she found it easier to draw pictures than spell words, for this is how Centaurs write. Penny thought it was similar to ancient Egyptian writing called hieroglyphics.

Penny decided to try things Sophie's way, so drew a picture of her new pupil and then asked her to write her name under it. This seemed to work well, and soon Sophie could write complete sentences. It was getting late. Penny decided to end lessons for the evening as the light was failing.

She gave her new friend some homework to do by leaving her a picture book of *Little Red Riding Hood* to try and read and an exercise to match the pictures to the words describing them. For example, if Sophie saw a wolf in the picture she was to underline the word 'wolf' on the page.

'There's one thing I would really love more than anything,' said Sophie. 'Can I have a real school uniform?'

Penny said she would do her best to get one from Mrs Dogberry, the school matron. They said good-bye and Sophie scratched Patch's neck underneath his mane. He in turn scratched her on the back of her neck as ponies do when they are best friends. Penny hopped up on to him and they flew over the treetops towards the school.

She landed him in his field with the other ponies, then took off his bridle and watched him trot away into the twilight to join them.

The light was still on in H.Q., so Penny decided to pay Potty Smythe a visit and tell her about Sophie and her plan to find Pip's parents.

The headmistress was going through some arrangements for the parents' day with the Fitznicelys, who were in charge of their invisible part of the event.

Penny knocked on the door and it opened of its own accord.

'Ah, here's Penny,' said Potty Smythe. 'And how is your new pupil?'

The Fitznicelys had already told her about Sophie. The headmistress had never seen a Centaureen either so was excited about the new arrival.

'She's going to help me find Pip's lost parents,' said Penny.

Potty Smythe swallowed hard. She was never too surprised by Penny's adventures but this could be a tough one.

'Lovely,' said the headmistress, trying not to sound too alarmed. 'I hope you can find them by parents' day. It would be wonderful for poor Pip, but how do you intend to do this, Princess Penny?'

'Sophie says that a creature called a Kelpie may have stolen them. I was going to ask you if I could be excused from school for a while so we could go to Equitopia to find out.'

Potty Smythe looked worried now.

'Kelpies are very dangerous, Penny,' she said. 'I know you can fight off Devlipeds, but these things are very tricky. They can change shape and it's awfully hard to identify one. But maybe King Valentine Silverwings can help. There might be an extra gift he can give you that enables you to see through their disguises. It's very brave of you to offer to find Mr and Mrs Horsington-Charmers but you are going to need his help.'

The Fitznicelys agreed.

'Sophie and I will call in at the Unicorn Palace before we start the search,' said Penny. 'I will need his blessing if I am to take on a new quest anyway.'

'When are you planning to go and for how long?' asked the headmistress.

'It all depends on Sophie,' said Penny.

After their chat Penny made her way back to the

dormitory where she shared a room with Sam and Pip.

They were sitting on Pip's bed going through photographs of their parents. Pip kept hers in an old shoebox together with other treasures. Sam had an album of her early pony days with her parents. Mr and Mrs Hedges looked young and brave. Penny noticed that Diana, Sam's mum, looked plumper than usual in one photograph at a Boxing Day meet.

'That was me!' laughed Sam. 'Mummy rode until her tummy got too big. My father stopped her because he said he did not want his child born in a muddy field or in the back of the horsebox!'

Pip's parents were tall and slim. Being vets, there were lots of photos of them with their patients. There was a lovely one of them either side of Pip on Waggit at a show. Pip was holding a huge trophy with loads of rosettes around her waist.

In the box was the article from *Horse and Hound* about their disappearance two years ago. Potty Smythe had read it at the time and taken Pip in as a scholarship girl at Fetlocks. She had no other living relatives except her Uncle Wally, a sailor based in the West Indies. If Pip had gone to live with him she would have lost Waggit as well. As her uncle was always at sea he had no place for ponies, so Pip would have ended up in a boarding school anyway.

Pip's eyes misted over as she pulled a silver locket out of the box. It was in the shape of a horseshoe on a silver chain. Opening it up, she showed it to her two friends. It had a picture of her parents inside and was inscribed *To Pip and Waggit with love from Mummy and Daddy*.

Sam and Penny put their arms around her.

'I know my parents are gone for ever,' said Sam. 'It's been hard and I've had to get used to it, but it's far worse for you, Pip, because you simply don't know what's happened to yours.'

'Don't give up hope,' said Penny. 'Who knows, someone may find them one day.' Silently she hoped that person would be Princess Penny, Unicorn Princess of Equitopia.

Mrs Honeybun, the school cook, put her head round the door. She was carrying a tray with three mugs of hot cocoa and some yummy home-made chocolate brownies for the girls.

'Now then, young ladies,' she said, beaming. 'You're all very quiet tonight.'

Just then Zack and Alice, Potty Smythe's two deer-hounds, bounded into the room, knocked the tray of brownies and mugs out of Mrs Honeybun's hand

and scoffed the lot. They cleaned up by licking all the cocoa off the floor. Mrs Honeybun sank on to a bed in fits of giggles. The two hounds thought this was even better entertainment and joined her on the duvet, licking her all over to thank her for their late-night snack. Everyone burst out laughing.

The girls eventually got to bed and fell asleep with the comforting thought that it was almost impossible to be sad at Fetlocks Hall for long.

CHAPTER FOUR

Sophie Goes to School

In the morning, after breakfast, Penny went to find Mrs Dogberry, the school matron, in the laundry room. She was busy mending a pile of school socks.

'My work is never done,' she sighed, setting down her darning needle as Penny slid rather stealthily into the room. 'What be you after, young lady? Caught your pants on a nail, I suppose!'

'Not this time,' laughed Penny. 'I've come to ask a

special favour, Mrs Dogberry. Have you got an old school uniform about my size going spare?'

'I might have,' said the school matron. 'Depends on what it's for.'

'Err,' said Penny, thinking quickly. 'It's for a friend to dress up in.'

'Oh, kind of fancy dress party, I suppose,' said Mrs Dogberry.

Penny just smiled. She could not possibly say, 'Well, actually it's for my friend who is half pony but wants to be a schoolgirl.'

Mrs Dogberry fumbled about in a wardrobe at the back of the laundry room and came up with a Fetlocks Hall school blazer, skirt, shirt, tie and a boater hat.

'What size shoes?' she asked.

'Oh, don't worry about the shoes,' said Penny. 'She's got some.'

In fact Sophie had four silver ones, but Penny could not tell Mrs Dogberry that.

'Thanks awfully, Matron,' said Penny as Mrs Dogberry folded up the uniform and put it into a carrier bag for her. 'My friend will love this.'

'Bring it back when she's finished with it, dear,' said the kind Mrs Dogberry, but Penny was halfway out of the door with the bag by then.

Today was not a lessons day for Penny. Scholarship children at Fetlocks Hall had to work on the yard four days a week and only had three days for school work. They had to be very quick learners – that was part of the requirements for a scholarship to the school.

The ponies had already been fed before breakfast so now it was time to complete all the yard duties and exercise them. Ben Faloon, stable boy and second-in-command to Henry, was soaking sugar beet in a large tub when Penny came into the feed room, carrying the bag.

'Good morning, Pony Pen,' he greeted her in his soft Irish accent. Ben came from County Cork. His father, Willy, was a famous racehorse trainer.

'I hope your mum and dad are coming to the parents' day,' said Penny. She missed the Faloons terribly and had not seen them since she'd helped Ben's racehorse, Scudeasy, to win the Grand National with the help of Lady Fitznicely's ghostly bloomers for blinkers.

'You could not keep the old ones out!' said Ben with a grin. 'I hear tell there's a horse show on the cards so I'm going to make a real Irish working hunter course for you all to jump round. Sure, there's a nice little hill in the park. It'll make an excellent Irish bank for your ponies to negotiate.'

Pip and Sam came in carrying paint cans and wearing boiler suits splattered with white paint.

'Henry's got us painting stables,' said Sam, handing Penny a boiler suit. 'She says they've got to be spick and span before the parents' bash.'

'She's sent old Mr Pennypot to raid the school gardens for plants for the flower baskets,' said Pip. 'The yard will look like Royal Ascot on Ladies' Day by the time we're finished.'

Penny put on the boiler suit and followed her two friends out into the sunshine. Carlos and Dom were already washing down walls with the power hose.

'You want a wave?' laughed Carlos, turning the hose on Dom.

Dom, being a surfer, was used to big splashes so he neatly stepped out of the way behind a door. Unfortunately, Henry was bustling past on the phone to the vet and got a complete soaking!

'*UUGH!*' she screamed, turning towards the children, looking like a drowned rat with her eye make-up running down her face in little black rivers. 'You horrible boy! It took me ages to do my hair and make-up this morning!'

Peter Fixcannon, who was on the other end of the phone, felt the full blast of this outburst and wondered what he had said to deserve such a remark.

'Errr . . . It's not you, Pete,' Henry blurted out. 'It's blinking Carlos – he's just power-hosed me!'

Peter Fixcannon burst into fits of laughter. He said he was on his way to Fetlocks Hall to X-ray Mandy Drafus's pony and would be there shortly.

Poor Henry had put on her prettiest make-up and fixed her unruly thick dark brown hair because her dream vet was visiting the yard that morning. Now she was dripping wet! She plonked herself down on an upturned bucket and giggled.

Carlos apologised and fetched her a towel from the tack room. Penny tried to wipe Henry's face with some tissues from her pocket but it only made it worse. Sam decided to dry her hair with the stable hairdryer usually used for the ponies' wet legs.

The result was not good. Henry's hair went so frizzy it was as if she'd had an electric shock and her face looked like it had been smeared with soot.

Just then Peter Fixcannon's van pulled into the yard.

'Henry, you look as though you have blown a fuse!' he laughed.

Henry laughed too. She did see the funny side of it, which made her feel a lot better.

By eleven o'clock the girls had painted the inside walls of four loose boxes shimmering white. It was time to exercise the ponies so Penny walked across the park with its great oak trees to find Patch. Budget was dozing in the shade of one of them with her daughter.

'Was that creature I saw in the woods a Centaureen?' she said as Penny passed.

'Yes,' replied Penny. 'She's called Sophie. She wants to go to school here.'

'Does she want to learn dressage, showjumping and polo?' asked Budget.

'No,' said Penny, 'she wants to learn human stuff like reading, writing and arithmetic.'

'Oh dear,' said Budget. 'When is she coming?'

'I'm giving her private lessons after school,' said Penny. 'She'll never come to classes here.'

'How are you going to stop her if she really wants to?' snorted Budget.

Penny had to confess she did not know but was certain Sophie was happy with the current arrangement.

The daily routine of caring for the ponies went by until the evening, when Penny and Patch flew over to

Middlemarsh Wood carrying Sophie's uniform. The little Centaureen's eyes lit up when she saw her new clothes. Penny helped her try them on. They fitted perfectly but she did look very strange. Instead of a normal girl's legs coming out below the skirt there was a nice pair of pony shoulders followed by the rest of its body.

Sophie and Penny wandered over to a pond in the clearing. Sophie gazed down at her reflection and looked very pleased with herself.

'Thank you so much, Penny,' she said, smiling. 'I really feel the part now.'

Penny checked the homework she had given Sophie. She had got most of the spelling right but had drawn more strange pictures all over the book.

'I did not think it was a very good story,' Sophie said, 'so I have rewritten it. You see, the girl in the red hood should never have allowed her grandmother to be eaten by that wolf. She should have shot the beast immediately with an arrow straight through its heart or cut its head off with her sword.'

Penny had to agree but said it would have made the story a very short one.

'What are you teaching me tonight?' asked Sophie, folding up her pony legs, settling down next to Patch and eating a handful of grass.

'I thought we'd try some simple arithmetic by learning numbers. It's called numeracy,' said Penny.

'Ah, you mean necromancy,' said Sophie.

'I think that means a kind of magic,' said Penny.

'Same thing,' replied Sophie.

Penny thought Henry Digit, head of maths, would agree with this comment, but Penny found it hard to see the comparison.

Penny wrote down all the numbers up to one hundred so Sophie could see what they looked like. She pointed to each figure and then spelt its name underneath it. Sophie repeated all the numbers after her very quickly, causing an extraordinary thing to happen. A large stone appeared in the clearing with a sword stuck in it.

'What's that!' said Penny.

'It's Excalibur, the sword of King Arthur,' replied Sophie.

'How did it get here?' asked Patch.

'By necromancy,' laughed Sophie. 'If I put certain magic numbers together I can make things appear. Those necro-numerals in that order will summon Excalibur.'

She said all the numbers very quickly backwards and the sword in the stone disappeared.

Penny and Patch looked at each other in

amazement. Perhaps it was not a good idea to teach Sophie maths at all in case any more unexpected visions appeared. It seemed clear that Sophie did not have a mind like a human or a pony but very much one of her own. Penny and Patch said goodbye to Sophie, who said she had a surprise for them tomorrow.

'I wonder what she's planning,' said Patch as they flew back to the Hall.

'Whatever it is, I don't think it'll be very straight-forward!' said Penny.

She was absolutely right.

Early the next day, Sophie, wearing her school uniform, trotted up the front steps to Fetlocks Hall and seated herself, as best she could, at the back of Henry Digit's maths class! True to her promise, she remained invisible to anyone but Penny, who gave a helpless gasp when she saw Sophie in the classroom.

'Surprise, surprise!' giggled Sophie. 'I'm a real pupil at last, thanks to you, Penny!'

Thank goodness nobody else could hear any of this. Penny thought it best to sit next to Sophie in case of an emergency. She smiled at her new friend sitting there excitedly, ears pricked, jotter at the ready and raring to go.

Henry Digit marched into the room with his spectacles poised on the end of his nose.

'Good morning, class,' he said, putting his notes down on his desk. 'Today we are continuing with algebra.' He scribbled a formula on the blackboard. 'Now, can someone tell me what x equals?'

Sophie immediately raised her hand but of course he could not see it.

Gig stuck her hand up and said, 'y squared.'

'Correct,' said the teacher.

Sophie gave Penny a worried look.

'That's rubbish,' she gasped so that only Penny could hear. 'In this case x equals . . . '

At this moment there was a loud thunderclap right on top of the building. It made everyone jump. Henry Digit's glasses fell off and he dropped his piece of chalk. Lucy Pinny screamed – she was terrified of storms.

'That was a bit unexpected,' said Mr Digit, picking up his chalk and replacing his spectacles.

'Best you don't try to answer the questions just yet,' said Penny under her breath to Sophie as kindly as she could. Goodness knows what Sophie would conjure up for square roots or logarithms!

Biology with Mrs Plant was even more unusual. Sophie was fascinated with the life cycle of frogs.

She told Penny she knew personally the frog the teacher had brought to school in a jam jar. He was once a very arrogant prince that a friend of hers had kissed just to put him in his place. As far as she was concerned he deserved all he was getting!

Penny thought this was very funny and stuck her tongue out at the frog.

'Are you all right, Penny dear?' asked Mrs Plant.

Miss Chaucer's history class on the Ancient Greeks was too much for Sophie.

'She's got it all wrong!' she told Penny. 'If it wasn't for us Centaurs giving the Greeks the idea of the Trojan Horse, Troy would never have fallen and the Trojans would have ruled for much longer!'

Lunchtime did not come soon enough.

Sophie had never eaten human food. She lived on a vegetarian diet of grass, berrymunders and herbs. She was determined to eat Mrs Honeybun's cottage pie, chips and peas followed by summer pudding and cream. Penny was not sure this was a good idea as she did not know whether Sophie's intestines were human or equine. Sophie had made her mind up to give it a go so Penny piled her plate high with extra lunch.

'You're hungry today, Penny,' said Mrs Honeybun, serving her with a huge portion of cottage pie. Penny picked up another knife and fork and shared her lunch with Sophie.

The result was terrible! Sophie obviously had a pony tummy and it was not made to cope with this kind of food. She galloped out of the refectory and through the great hall, jumped the main entrance steps and raced down on to the front lawn, where the Fitznicelys were having a picnic lunch.

'Oh my goodness!' said Lady Sarah as Sophie collapsed in the middle of the quail egg and cucumber sandwiches.

'The poor thing's got colic!' shouted Antonia.

Penny was running towards them as fast as her legs could carry her, looking very worried.

'Don't let her roll,' commanded Sir Walter, 'or she will twist her gut and die!'

'Penny,' said Arabella, 'this is an emergency! Run for your Unicorn Tears and Antonia and I will sit on her head to stop her rolling!'

Penny did a U-turn and raced back up the steps. The third one instantly sprang open and the vial of Unicorn Tears leapt into her hand.

She sped back to the lawn, where poor Sophie was screaming with pain and trying violently to roll like a pony with bad colic. Arabella and Antonia and their father were pinning her head and neck to the ground to stop her turning over. Quickly Penny trickled a drop of Unicorn Tears down Sophie's throat and the pain healed instantly.

Sophie got up on her four legs and gave Penny a hug.

'I have been very silly,' she said. 'Thank you, Penny, for saving my life. I have been mistaken. This proves I cannot possibly live the life of a human! I wanted to go to school so much, but it's clear I just don't fit in because I am an ugly Centaureen!' With that she burst into tears.

'My dear,' said Lady Sarah, stroking Sophie's golden back. 'You are the most beautiful creature I have ever seen, and not ugly at all!'

The others all agreed.

'Sophie,' said Penny wisely, 'we are all what we are. You are not a girl and not a pony – you are a Centaureen and should be so proud of it.'

Sophie stopped crying and thought for a moment. Slowly, a big smile lit up her pretty face.

'You are absolutely right,' she beamed. 'You have all been so kind. Whatever can I do to thank you?'

'Well,' said Penny, 'we'd all really appreciate it if you would come to Equitopia with me to help find Pip's lost parents as soon as possible.'

'Poor little Pip,' said Sir Walter. 'Everyone would love her to see her mama and papa again.'

'It shall be done!' said Sophie. 'Penny, tell Aunt Portia we are going tonight. I will come for you at midnight and we will fly to the entrance of Equitopia at the Great White Horse of Wiltshire.'

CHAPTER FIVE

Equitopian Underbelly

Patch was disappointed he was not going with Penny and Sophie to Equitopia. Penny did not know how long they would be away and it might look funny if Patch simply disappeared for a while. Henry would be worried for a start and his pony friends would miss him.

An anxious Potty Smythe told Penny to be careful as anything to do with Kelpies would be a dangerous mission. However, Penny was ready with her Lance of Courage tucked into her waistband, the vial of Unicorn Tears in her pocket and Queen Starlight's Horn placed between the second and third buttons of her blazer.

At midnight she stood ready and waiting on the school steps with the headmistress and the Fitznicelys as Sophie cantered across the lawn towards her from the wood. The Centaureen looked quite different now. Gone were the school uniform and the plaits. Her long shining blonde hair streaked down to her pony knees. Around her waist was a belt with a sword and a dagger attached. Her bow and quiver of arrows were slung around her back. She had a leather armband on each forearm and she was wearing a black and gold crown.

'You look really cool, Sophie!' said Penny, feeling underdressed in her school uniform. 'Is the crown a real one or just for show?'

'You'll see,' replied Sophie as Penny vaulted on to her back and wrapped a school scarf around the Centaureen's waist so she had something to hang on to.

'Good luck, both of you,' said Potty Smythe.

'Take care,' said the Fitznicelys.

'*Let's Fly!*' said Penny.

They waved goodbye as Sophie rose into the air and then flew away into the night sky.

On the way Sophie explained that the part of Equitopia where she and other enchanted ponies lived was called the Underbelly. Although the unicorns ruled all of Equitopia they rarely visited that province.

Soon they were flying over the rolling green hills of Wiltshire. The moon was bright enough to see the Great White Horse with his big round eye, which formed the entrance to Equitopia, from quite a long way away.

Penny landed Sophie neatly beside it. The Centaureen trotted around the eye three times to the right and halfway round to the left. Then she knelt down in the centre of it with Penny on her back. Two silver horseshoe-like handles appeared in the turf and she grabbed hold of them with both hands.

'OPEN EQUITOPIA,' they commanded together.

The eye started to shake and lifted itself free of the earth. A shaft of glittering light shot out of the hole revealed in the ground.

'OK, let's go, Princess Penny,' said Sophie as she leapt down into the tunnel of light.

'*Whee!*' said an excited Penny, hanging on to the school scarf and trying not to swallow mouthfuls of palomino hair streaming out behind her friend.

They flew out of the eye of a similar white horse on the Equitopian side of the tunnel into a silvery landscape covered in snow. The last time Penny had been here for her coronation, the fields were as green as those of Terrestequinus.

'*Brrr*,' shivered Sophie. 'It is winter here and very chilly. That's another reason why I left for your world.'

'You would not like our winters either,' said Penny, looking at the snowy landscape. 'They are grey and wet with thick mud.'

They flew over the glistening white fields and frozen lakes until they found the river of stars leading to a massive plunging waterfall.

'*Aagh!*' said Sophie. 'This is going to be freezing! Are you ready, Penny?'

Penny could not remember getting wet at all the last time she plunged down this waterfall on King Valentine Silverwings' back, but that was because he had unicorn magic.

'I'll try to make it as quick as possible,' said Penny, flying Sophie out over the edge of the falls and gently descending until she saw the curtain of watery stars, the entrance to the unicorn's palace, about half-way down.

'OK,' she said, 'here's the way in. The quicker we get through, the drier we will be, so I'll count one, two, three, go and let's shoot through it as fast as we can fly!'

On the word 'go', Sophie was through in a flash so they hardly got wet at all. Both of them laughed as they landed in the huge crystal cavern of the palace. The unicorns came trotting over, flapping their beautiful white wings. They parted and knelt down on one knee to make way for their king.

'My dear Princess Penny,' said King Valentine, strolling over and nuzzling her cheek.

'Your Majesty,' said Penny, giving a graceful curtsy. 'Allow me to introduce my friend Sophie.'

Sophie bowed on one knee like the unicorns.

'Oh, I know Princess Sophie,' said the King. 'How are you, my dear, and your parents, King Rufus and Queen Amazon?'

Penny's mouth fell open. Sophie's crown was real. She had no idea she was PRINCESS of the Centaurs!

'We are all well, sire,' said Sophie, rising to her four feet.

King Valentine tossed his graceful head to one side and a small unicorn flew over, bearing Penny's own crown on a sparkling gold cushion with tassels.

'Kneel, child,' said the King. Penny did so and he placed the crown on her head. 'Arise, Princess Penny, Equitopia Regina Electa,' he said, smiling.

Penny stood up straight and puffed out her chest. She loved wearing her dazzling crown – it made her feel like a real princess. She wished she could take it back to school with her but King Valentine would not allow it. He said it was too precious and must stay in Equitopia.

'Oh, Penny!' said Sophie. 'It's beautiful, all gold and silver with diamond stars. It makes my own look very dull.'

'Yours is a Centaur's crown,' said King Valentine. 'You are a creature of strength, honour and great beauty so it is fitting it is made of black jet and gold lace. I know you are proud to wear it, Sophie.'

Sophie tried a curtsy like Penny's. She managed it quite well by crossing her front legs and keeping her back ones steady.

'Your Majesty,' said Penny, 'we have come to find my friend Pip's lost parents. They are equine vets and disappeared two years ago when they were studying zebras in Africa. Sophie thinks they may have been stolen by a Kelpie, so I've come to ask your permission to go with her to the Underbelly of Equitopia to find them.'

King Valentine Silverwings looked a little worried.

'Of course, Princess Penny,' said the King hesitantly. 'It is an interesting place. We unicorns don't go there very much. It can be quite dangerous, but I know you are well equipped to deal with Kelpies and the like. Kelpies are not what they seem, though, and play tricks on humans. I will give you permission, but you must not go into their creepy tower. They will not want you to discover their secrets and you will be in grave danger. You are lucky to have Sophie by your side. She knows something of their ways. I am always here to help and protect you both. If you need me, just blow my mother's Horn three times and I'll be there. I will keep an eye on your progress by looking into my crystal cloud.'

Penny thanked the King. She was looking forward to visiting the Underbelly but did not know what to expect. However, she felt more secure knowing he would be keeping watch over her. Penny curtsied and hopped on to Sophie's back.

The unicorns waved goodbye with their wings as the two princesses flew through the curtain of water stars and out into the snowy landscape.

'Which way?' asked Penny.

'We just follow the river until we reach the caves,' said Sophie. 'It will only take an hour flying like this but it would take me a day to get this far on my hoofs.'

'Your parents will be pleased to see you,' said Penny.

'Hmm,' said Sophie. 'I did not exactly tell them I was leaving, but it is expected of me to go on an adventure without notice.'

'They must be terribly worried!' said Penny.

'Centaurs are not like human parents,' said Sophie. 'They would not have allowed themselves to worry about me and have probably concentrated on my two brothers' archery and fencing lessons instead of caring about where I have been. I'm only a Centaureen. We are very rare because our mothers mostly have colts. We are not as valued as the boys. Centaurs are a bunch of back-slapping, swashbuckling, bragging heroes. They don't think much of us girls and tend to keep us out of their boyish world. I'd have to slay a Minotorse to get their approval,' said the Centaureen.

'What's that?' asked Penny.

'A terrifying creature,' shivered Sophie, 'half horse and half bull!'

Penny was glad she had brought her Lance of Courage and Queen Starlight's Horn with her. Devlipeds were bad enough but she did not like the sound of Minotorses at all!

They followed the river until it came to a mountain where the waters flowed through a set of three caves like the archways of a bridge. Penny and Sophie flew down and through one of the caves. It should have been very dark inside but the sparkling stars of the river lit the vaults above them with dancing blue and green lights.

Soon the river emerged from the caves into bright sunshine, blazing from a dazzling blue sky and reflecting on the snowy ground.

'Here we are,' said Sophie as they flew over a forest. 'This is the Equitopian Underbelly.'

A flock of what looked to Penny like pretty blue birds was fluttering below them. Penny took Sophie down for a closer look.

'They are tiny flying horses!' exclaimed Penny.

'Yes,' said Sophie with a smile. 'We call them Hairies.'

The Hairies were quite alarmed to see a flying Centaureen with a human child on her back, and dived out of the way.

'It's only me, Maddy,' Sophie shouted to the leader. 'Have you seen our herd?'

'I thought you were a Dragony, Sophie,' screamed poor little Maddy, who was about the size of a swallow. 'What are you doing up here? *Centaurs* can't fly!'

'But Unicorn Princesses can fly us,' said Sophie, pointing over her shoulder at Penny. 'Meet my friend, Princess Penny, Unicorn Princess of Equitopia.'

'Oh my goodness,' said the tiny Hairy in a very

squeaky high voice. 'I've heard of you, Your Royal Highness. You are the one who saved us all from the dastardly Devliped Plot to take over Terrestequinus and Equitopia. I am greatly honoured to meet you. Nice crown too!'

'I'm very pleased to meet you, Maddy,' said Penny. 'Sorry we scared you.'

'The rest of your herd has gone to the Pampos for a party, Sophie,' continued Maddy. 'Have you forgotten it's your brother Manus's birthday today?'

Sophie had forgotten.

'I've been away at school in Terrestequinus,' she said. 'I don't even know what day it is!'

'The poor little things,' said Penny as Maddy and the rest of her flock wheeled away. 'We must look like a jumbo jet to Hairies!'

'Lucky for them we weren't a Dragony,' said Sophie.

'Don't tell me,' said Penny. 'It's half dragon and half pony.'

'You've got it,' laughed Sophie. 'Terribly ugly things.'

The Pampos was a great flat grassland on the other side of the forest. The Centaurs loved the place and went there for holidays because there was lots of space to race about in and countless bushes of their favourite berrymunders.

Sophie and Penny headed in that direction. As

they flew over the outskirts of the forest Penny could see tracks in the snow left by many galloping horses. Sophie said to follow the hoof prints until they caught up with the rest of her herd.

'You'll probably hear them before you see them if they are having a party,' said Sophie. 'They are a raucous, noisy lot. I hope you won't be offended by them, Penny.'

Penny said she'd be fine and was sure Sophie's family would be delighted to see their daughter back safely. Sophie kept quiet. Knowing her family, she didn't bet on it!

It was not long before the sound of very loud rock music caught Penny's ears.

'I told you,' said Sophie. 'They are whooping it up down there. That's our own band, Hoofbash.'

The closest thing Penny had heard to it was a kind of music her older sister Charlotte called 'heavy metal'.

As they got nearer Penny could see there certainly was a party going on. The Centaurs had set up a stage for their band and made lots of bonfires to keep warm. The music was deafening but they all seemed to be enjoying it tremendously, galloping about wildly, bucking, kicking, rearing and prancing to the beat. On the stage were five Centaurs, bashing away at drums, guitar-like instruments, trumpets and saxophones. Penny decided to make a great entrance by landing Sophie right on the stage.

The result was amazing. The music stopped instantly and the fascinated Centaurs ceased careering about and crowded forward for a better look at the new arrivals. A large chestnut Centaur with a hairy chest, long red dreadlocks and huge beard fastened together with gold rings trotted towards the two princesses.

'Sophie!' he boomed, leaping up on to the stage in one bound. 'You're back! Come to your father, King Rufus of the Centaurs!'

Penny slipped off Sophie's back as the King grabbed his daughter, picked her up, and held her aloft for all to see.

The crowd of Centaurs roared, drew their bows and fired a curtain of arrows into the air as a salute. Sophie's two brothers, Manus and Rollo, leapt up to join them on stage to give their sister a hearty slap on the back.

The crowd parted to let her mother through. A wild but beautiful white Centauride came galloping towards them. She cleared several Centaurs with one massive leap to join her family on the stage.

'Our daughter has returned to tell us of her

courageous adventures and how many Minotorses she has slain!' boomed King Rufus.

Sophie looked rather annoyed. 'Well, actually, I haven't slain any. I ran away to Terrestequinus to go to school,' she said quietly.

There was a stony silence. King Rufus put Sophie down and stood frowning at her with his hands on his hips.

'I am disappointed in you, Sophie,' he said sternly. He turned towards the band, raised his arms and shouted, 'Let the music commence!'

'Wait!' said Sophie. 'You have forgotten my friend here, Princess Penny of Equitopia. If it wasn't for her I would not have returned. In fact, she saved my life.'

A deafening cheer rose up from the crowd. Penny felt very small among the Centaurs. Sophie's father was at least eighteen hands high. His whole height up to the top of his head from his hoofs must have been nearly four metres!

'Not *the* Princess Penny who can ride Devlipeds and challenged King Despot Dragontail to a duel with her Lance of Courage?'

'That's me,' said Penny.

'Well,' continued King Rufus, 'we have a real hero in our midst! Welcome, Princess Penny, to our herd.

We are honoured to have you as our guest and hope to hear stories of your brave adventures and conquests. Come and join the celebrations, for it is Prince Manus's birthday.'

With that he grabbed her and seated her on Manus's back. The noisy band started up again. The Centaurs whooped, yelled and resumed their mad dancing. Prince Manus leapt off the stage, carrying Penny, and joined in. She took hold of his wild black dreadlocks and held on tight. It was a good thing Penny could ride very well as he bucked and reared and cavorted about to the crazy music like a wild bronco!

Sophie was left standing on the stage, feeling quite forgotten. Her mother, Queen Amazon, seemed a little more concerned. She trotted up with a basket of berrymunders and handed it to her daughter.

'Oh well, better luck next time, daughter,' she said, patting Sophie on the head.

The music stopped. The Centaurs all cheered and clapped. Penny managed to slip off Manus's back and ran through the crowd to find her friend. Queen Amazon bowed as Penny approached. She noticed the Queen had a big, jagged scar on her hindquarters.

'That must have been a terrible wound,' said Penny.

'Oh, I carry it with pride,' said the Queen. 'That was from the first Minotorse I slew.'

Penny shuddered.

'My brothers have killed one each already,' said Sophie. 'Manus is sixteen and Rollo is only fourteen.'

Queen Amazon asked if Penny would be staying long.

'I'm here to find my friend's lost parents,' said Penny.

'It looks like the work of a Kelpie,' added Sophie, 'so I said I'd give her a hand.'

CHAPTER SIX

The Four Winds

Dusk was gathering and Penny was tired and hungry. They had decided not to spend the night with the Centaurs because Sophie said they would be dancing until dawn. The music would keep them awake and her family would want Penny to sit around their campfire for hours swapping tales of adventure. So they decided to move on towards the coast where the Kelpies lived. Sophie said she had some good friends there who would put them up for the night.

The grasslands of the Pampos gave way to sand dunes. The snow had not fallen there but the wind was wild and cold.

'Not far now,' said Sophie, pointing at what looked like a circus tent in the shelter of some large dunes below.

A soft light came from the entrance to the tent. The two princesses landed outside and Sophie trotted in with Penny on her back. They were welcomed into the warm cosy tent by four lovely Arabian horses. The floor was covered in Persian carpets and strewn with pretty silk cushions. The ceiling was dark blue and sparkled with many small lights glittering like stars.

'Hello, Sophie,' said a bay mare wearing a handsome red and gold velvet rug with a fur collar.

Sophie introduced Penny to her four friends who were named, in Arabic, after the four winds, Shimal (North), Janoub (South), Sharq (East) and Gharb (West).

'We are on our way to the sea to visit the Kelpies,' said Sophie. 'We have been flying all day since we left Terrestequinus. Please could we stay here with you tonight?'

The Arabian horses were delighted to see the princesses and said they were more than welcome to stay.

Penny slipped off Sophie's back and collapsed among the pretty cushions.

Sophie folded up her pony legs and stretched out beside her, propping herself up on one arm.

Gharb whinnied softly and a table appeared with all sorts of yummy things on it for Penny to eat. She tucked into saffron rice and raisins with a kind of spicy lamb and mint stew, followed by delicious pink Turkish delight.

Sophie had a bowl of berrymunders and herbs.

Sharq flicked her tail and conjured up some peaceful music, very different from the noise Hoofbash had been making earlier.

Janoub made a little twirl and a lovely pool with bubbles appeared in the floor of the tent with candles arranged around it and warm fluffy white towels.

'We thought you two would like a nice relaxing bath,' said Shimal, pouring some oil that smelt of rose petals into the water. 'I will get your clothes washed and ironed and ready to wear for the morning, Penny, but here is something for you to put on once you've had your bath.'

She produced a shimmering peacock-green silk robe with a fur lining. Penny could not believe her luck. After their bath the two princesses sank into the soft cushions and fell asleep.

Penny was so intrigued with her new magical Arabian friends that she dreamed of deserts and horses. She could hear a voice saying,

'And God took a handful of the South wind and from it formed a horse, saying:

> *I create thee, Oh Arabian.*
> *To thy forelock, I bind victory in battle.*
> *On thy back, I set a rich spoil*
> *and a treasure in thy loins.*
> *I establish thee as one of*
> *the glories of the Earth . . .*
> *I give thee flight without wings.'*

A warm wind from the desert blew on her face and Penny woke up to find Shimal breathing softly on her cheek.

'Wake up, Princess Penny,' she said. 'It's time for breakfast.'

Sophie was already up and sharpening her arrows because Shimal had caught the scent of a Minotorse and advised her to be careful.

'Hi, Penny,' she said. 'You slept well!'

Penny told the others about her dream.

'Ah,' said Gharb. 'You have dreamed of how Allah made Arabian horses. He created them from the four winds. Spirit from the North, Strength from the South, Speed from the East and Intelligence from the West. We four are those same horses of the wind from which all Arab horses stem. Now here's some lovely porridge and stewed apple to make you as strong as we are!'

Penny liked Sophie's friends very much. She thanked them for their hospitality and tucked into the porridge.

'The Bedouins, a great horse-loving nomadic people of the desert, called the first Arabian horse "Drinker of the Wind",' added Sharq. 'The Queen of Sheba gave King Solomon a beautiful mare called Safanad. He also owned a stallion called Zad el-Raheb. The children of these two horses are legendary. It is said that anyone who owns one of their descendants will possess special gifts of communication with horses.'

Penny told them about her friend Matt, who had an Arab called Shaab. The Four Winds looked at each other and smiled.

'Your friend is very lucky,' said Janoub, 'for Shaab is the prefix or forename given to all of that family. He is the owner of a legend and will be a gifted child.'

Penny wondered if Matt knew this or if he had just been keeping it quiet. He was a really good rider but was there something more? She knew he could not speak Equalese but maybe he had some sort of telepathy with horses, a bit like a horse whisperer.

It was time to go. Sophie slung her bow and quiver with her newly sharpened arrows over her back and Penny hopped up. They said goodbye to the four horses, who breathed a gust of wind and blew them on their way.

CHAPTER SEVEN

Kelpie Towers

The two princesses flew down to the sea and followed the coastline until Sophie pointed at a jagged inlet. The waves crashed wildly on the rocks and sprayed high up the cliff face. They glided down the inlet towards the land, finally reaching a ruined tower on a tall rock with the sea churning around its base.

Sitting on the rock were a number of small green ponies with webbed fin-like feet. Their manes and tails were made of seaweed. Some of them were playing in the water, diving and surfacing like seals.

'Here we are,' said Sophie as Penny landed them on the safest part of the slimy rock she could find. 'Kelpie Towers. This is where the Kelpies hang out when they are not up to mischief somewhere else.' She pointed up at the ruined tower surrounded by crashing waves. 'They keep children's time-frozen parents in that tower until they decide to use them to trap the child. Nobody has ever dared to go inside or tried to free any parents in case the Kelpies try the same trick on them. Here is the best place to see them in their true form because Kelpies can change their shape as easily as a chameleon changes its colour.'

Moving like seals, the Kelpies flipped over the rocks to greet Sophie and Penny.

One of them offered Penny a webbed fin to help her down.

'Don't touch them,' whispered Sophie. 'They are very sticky. If you get stuck to one it will carry you beneath the waves and drown you.'

Cautiously, Penny slipped off Sophie, her hand on the Lance of Courage tucked into her waistband.

'Good morning, Sophie,' said a Kelpie, instantly turning into a wrinkled old fishwife. 'Quite an entrance. I did not know you could fly now. Would you and your friend like to come into Kelpie Towers for a cup of tea? Look, your friends are already here.'

Penny was amazed. The other Kelpies had turned themselves into The Fetlocks Hall Flyers! Sam, Pip, Dom and Matt and Carlos ran over to her.

'Don't take any notice,' said Sophie, placing herself between Penny and the children. 'They are not real. The Kelpies are just playing tricks on you. Banjax,' said Sophie to the old hag, 'this is Princess Penny of Equitopia so you can just stop doing that. Her powers are greater than yours and she can see straight through you!'

In a flash the Kelpies resumed their normal shapes.

'Oh,' said Banjax, who seemed to be the leader of the clan. 'Well, that's different. We are very pleased to welcome you to Kelpie Towers, Your Highness. To what do we owe the honour of your visit?'

Penny straightened her crown and stepped forward.

'I have come with a special request,' she began tactfully. 'I believe that you may know something about the disappearance of my friend Philippa Horsington-Charmers' parents. They went missing from Africa two years ago. I am asking for your help to find them as I wish to bring them back to Terrestequinus.'

The Kelpies murmured among each other.

'It wasn't us,' said a small one, not much bigger

than a foal. 'It would have been the Zebra Kelpies from Zulupopo.'

Penny glanced at the tower. She thought the Kelpies were fibbing and that Pip's parents were hidden somewhere inside it. Penny asked if they could return them.

The Kelpies huddled together, muttering to each other as if they were plotting something.

'Of course we can,' said Banjax with a sly smile, 'but it will take us a couple of days. When you get home, bring Pip down to the nearest beach and we'll see her parents are delivered.'

Penny was delighted, but Sophie, who knew them much better, was not convinced. This was all too easy – Kelpies were usually very tricky.

'I don't have to remind you of how important my friend Penny is,' she told the clan leader. 'No tricks now, or you might end up stripped of your own powers!'

'I'm sure the Kelpies will honour their promise,' said Penny, who was not sure if she had any power-stripping abilities. However, she knew a unicorn who did and he was watching the Kelpies' every move at this very moment in his crystal cloud.

'We should be back at Fetlocks Hall shortly,' said Penny.

'We'll be waiting for you whenever you bring the child to the seaside,' said Banjax.

Penny thanked the Kelpies. She and Sophie were very pleased to be leaving that wild, cold place.

'You'll have to be on your guard, Penny,' said Sophie as they flew inland towards the forest. 'I don't trust them at all. I've never heard of the Zebra Kelpies of Zulupopo for a start!'

The snow had started falling again, causing Penny and Sophie to shiver. It blew up into a blizzard, so Penny thought it safer to land somewhere. Sophie said she knew of a cave they could shelter in not far below. They decided to settle in a clearing and build a fire in the cave to keep warm until the snowstorm was over. The cave was frequently used by wandering Centaurs and had a good stock of dry twigs and branches stored inside the entrance.

'How are we going to light it?' asked Penny between chattering teeth as Sophie stacked the twigs in a wigwam shape.

Sophie picked up a flint and put it by the dry wood. She gave it a sharp tap with one of her silver shoes to make a spark and the fire burst into life. They sat warming their hands and discussing their adventure so far.

Suddenly Sophie got to her feet and pricked her ears.

Something else was sheltering in that cave.

Penny gasped and pointed at the wall. The shadow of a huge horse with the torso of a man but the head of a bull with massive horns loomed towards them.

Penny reached for her Lance of Courage as the thing roared and leapt out of the darkness straight at her. She stood up and took a step backwards but tripped on a rock, stumbling to the ground as the creature pounced. As she fell, the little silver cane dropped out of her hand and bounced away. In a panic, she fumbled around but could not find it, so she reached for Queen Starlight's Horn, knowing its music would calm the beast. Before she could put the instrument to her lips, however, there was a terrible groan and a huge thud as the Minotorse hit the ground next to her. She rolled out of the way, retrieving her Lance and pointing it at the creature's head. The Lance did not take on its usual defensive shape and shoot out its deadly blue flashes. There was no need, for the danger was over and the creature lay still on the floor of the cave, an arrow sticking out of its mighty chest.

Penny glanced up at the Centaureen standing tall with her bow still poised. Sophie had slain her first Minotorse!

The two princesses gazed at each other.

'You saved my life, Sophie,' whispered Penny. 'You are a true Centauride and a brave princess!'

Sophie walked over to the dead Minotorse. She gave it a prod with her front hoof. It did not move.

'It's real!' she exclaimed, pulling her arrow out of its heart. 'Do you know, Penny, for a moment I thought it was a Kelpie playing a trick!'

CHAPTER EIGHT

Back to
School

Sophie pulled out her sword, struck off one of the Minotorse's horns and tucked it into her belt.

'I will have to take my parents something to prove I slew the thing,' she said, 'as I have no battle wounds to show off.'

'I will tell them how you saved me,' said Penny.

'Surely preventing someone from being killed by one of those things means a lot?'

'Saving a Unicorn Princess is pretty good going too,' said Sophie, smiling.

The snowstorm had stopped. Sophie and Penny flew over the white treetops until they spotted smoke rising from another clearing. They descended to find Sophie's herd recovering from the party.

King Rufus, Rollo and Manus were building a huge bonfire. They were drinking cups of hot berrymunder tea and looking a little tired. Queen Amazon was stirring a huge cauldron of the stuff and handing it out to some other slightly groggy-looking Centaurs.

Sophie and Penny trotted proudly over to the King.

Holding her sword over her head, Sophie pulled the Minotorse's horn out of her belt and threw it at her father's feet. King Rufus picked it up and held it aloft.

'Brothers and sisters,' he boomed. 'I have wonderful news. Princess Sophie has slain her first Minotorse! See, she has brought us one of its horns to prove it!'

Sophie's mother and the rest of the herd cantered

over. A huge cheer went up as King Rufus and his Queen hugged their daughter.

'Sophie is the bravest Centaureen of them all,' cried Penny, 'because she saved me from the beast. If it wasn't for her, Equitopia would not have a ruling princess. I owe her my life and King Valentine Silverwings himself will be proud of her.'

The Centaurs gave an even louder cheer. King Rufus, Rollo and Manus hoisted Sophie up on to their strong shoulders and carried her around the glade at a mad gallop. The rest of the herd joined in, whooping and hollering.

Penny was beginning to miss Patch and the rest of The Flyers by now and was ready to go back to Fetlocks. There was important work to do. She was looking forward to reuniting Pip with her lost parents, but it was too risky to tell her in case the Kelpies *were* playing some kind of trick and had no intention of delivering Mr and Mrs Horsington-Charmers at all. There was also the parents' day show to prepare for.

It seemed impossible that so much had happened in such a short time. After all, she had only been away for two days. Now Sophie seemed happy with her family, Penny thought she would want to stay in the Underbelly for ever, but Sophie would not hear of it.

'I owe you so much, Penny,' she said, 'because you have proved to me that I am a true Centaureen and not a girl or a pony. You have made me proud of who I am. I cannot let you complete the rest of this quest alone as I really don't trust the Kelpies, so I am coming back to Terrestequinus with you to help in any way I can.'

Penny thanked Sophie and they stood holding hands as the herd of Centaurs galloped around them shouting, 'Bravo for Princess Sophie and Princess Penny of Equitopia!'

They decided to call in at the palace on the way home to say goodbye to the unicorns.

King Valentine Silverwings was delighted to see the two princesses safely returned from the Underbelly.

Of course he knew exactly what had happened on their adventure because he'd been watching the story unfold in his crystal cloud. He had to admit he'd been anxious when Penny fell over and dropped her Lance of Courage, but he knew his mother's Horn would have worked just as well and tamed the beast, even if Sophie had not been so quick with her arrow.

'I have a present for you, Sophie,' he said, handing her a golden box.

Sophie's eyes lit up as she opened it to find a beautiful golden unicorn pendant with diamond eyes on a gold chain. When she turned it over she found an inscription on the back.

To Her Royal Highness Princess Sophie of the Centaurs for her bravery in saving the life of Princess Penny, one hundredth Unicorn Princess of Equitopia.

'Oh, sire,' she said. 'It's beautiful! Thank you a thousand times! Please put it around my neck and it shall stay there for ever.'

King Valentine did as he was asked and Penny applauded loudly. The other unicorns clapped their wings together and Sophie made the most graceful curtsy she could.

King Valentine and the unicorns escorted the two princesses back to the Equitopian White Horse. Although the snow was still on the ground they could see him quite clearly outlined in silver.

The King said he was looking forward to parents' day. He would be watching it all in his crystal cloud and hoped it would be a huge success. He was pleased Sophie was going to be at Penny's side when

Pip's parents were delivered because he did not trust the Kelpies either. He warned Penny to stay on her guard.

'Don't forget to call for me with my mother's Horn if you get into trouble,' he told Penny as she handed him back her precious crown for safe keeping.

The two princesses took their leave and sped down the tunnel of light. They shot out of the Great White Horse's eye on the Terrestequinus side and away into the midnight sky above the Wiltshire downs.

'Back to school!' cried Penny as they zoomed over the hills towards Dorset.

In the early hours of the morning, they landed on the gravel drive of Fetlocks Hall at the base of the stone steps. Potty Smythe was waiting for them with the deerhounds, terriers, and her two pet unicorns, Hippolita and Rain, who had told her when to expect the princesses.

'Welcome back, you two,' she said, smiling. 'How did you get on? Any news of the lost parents?'

Penny and Sophie told her everything that had happened over a cup of tea and a plate of Mrs Honeybun's wonderful bacon and egg sandwiches in H.Q.

Sophie munched on her own supply of

berrymunders that she'd packed into her quiver. After her last experience of eating human food she was not going to try it again.

'We'll have to get Pip down to the coast somehow without giving away the secret just in case the Kelpies pull a fast one,' said the headmistress.

'What about a beach picnic ride?' said Penny. 'We can take the ponies down there in the lorries.'

Potty Smythe thought this was a great idea and said she would arrange everything for the day after tomorrow. The headmistress then filled them in on what had happened while they had been away. Preparations for parents' day were going well and Matt's horse had arrived from Dubai.

Penny told Potty Smythe what the Four Winds had said about Matt and Shaab.

'It would not surprise me,' said Miss Manning-Smythe. 'I think Matt has been keeping very quiet and knows a lot more about the magical life of horses than he lets on.'

'What's new?' said Arabella and Antonia, walking straight through the wall of the study.

Sophie showed them her pendant and told them how she slew the Minotorse.

'Crumbs!' said Arabella. 'Can we have a go with your bow and arrows?'

'Mama is arranging an archery display for the ghostly part of parents' day,' added Antonia. 'She does not trust us with the equipment ever since Arabella shot Count Blackdrax in the bottom when he was picking up a halfpenny he had dropped in the grass.'

'I don't know what the fuss was about,' said Arabella. 'The arrow went straight through him! The only thing that was hurt was his pride.'

Everyone laughed. It was good to be back at Fetlocks Hall.

Penny and Sophie were really tired. It had been a long two days. Sophie fell asleep on a rug in H.Q. and Penny climbed upstairs, accompanied by Arabella and Antonia, still asking questions. Eventually she arrived at the girls' dormitory, where her roommates, Pip and Sam, were curled up fast asleep.

Penny climbed into bed, glanced at Pip, and hoped against hope that her friend would see her parents soon.

'Where have you been?' asked Sam the next morning, sitting up in bed and rubbing her eyes.

'Potty Smythe told us you'd gone home on family business,' said Pip, coming out of their bathroom still scrubbing her teeth.

'Birthday party,' said Penny. 'How's the parents' day coming along?'

'Potty Smythe's arranged it for August the first after the Royal International Horse Show so that Carlos's dad, Don Frederico, can come. We've got two weeks to get ready,' said Pip with her mouth full of toothpaste.

Sam rummaged in the drawer of her bedside cabinet and handed Penny a typed piece of paper.

'Here's the schedule,' she said. 'Potty Smythe worked it out with all of us, including Henry and the other teachers. I think it looks pretty good.'

Penny read the order of events.

FETLOCKS HALL PONY SCHOOL
PARENTS' OPEN DAY
SCHEDULE OF EVENTS
9 a.m. Reception in the great hall for all parents, staff and children
Welcome speech by the headmistress
Refreshments
10 a.m. Tour of the school, classrooms and projects
11 a.m. Tour of the stable yard. Chance to meet the ponies
12 p.m. Working hunter competition in the park
1–2 p.m. Picnic on the lawn or lunch in the refectory, weather permitting

2 p.m. Pony club mounted games demonstration
2.30 p.m. Polo match
3 p.m. Dressage display
3.30 p.m. Puissance showjumping display
4 p.m. Display of Arab horsemanship by Matt Khareef
4.30 p.m. Theatrical display to music by Merc and Morri
Fangley-Fitznicely
5–5.30 p.m. Tea party in the great hall to finish

'Cool,' said Penny. 'We'll have to get practising. It's important we put on a good show for the grown-ups.'

After breakfast Arabella and Antonia handed Penny their own schedule for the parents' day. It was written by hand on an elegant invitation card with the Fetlocks Hall crest at the top. It read:

Sir Walter and Lady Sarah Fitznicely have great pleasure in inviting you to join them for an 'Invisible Parents' Day' at Fetlocks Hall

The ghostly events seemed to be happening at a similar time to the school ones but with periods allowed for the ghosts to haunt some of the children's displays.

They included a champagne breakfast at 10 a.m. in

the ballroom, a side-saddle display by the twins, an archery competition and sword-fighting display by Sir Walter and his brother-in-law, Sir Rupert de Parrott, and a music recital by The Headless Quartet!

There was a croquet match with tea to follow, a fashion parade and an evening party.

Penny was particularly amused by the proposed ghost-train ride around the park.

'Where are you going to get the train?' she asked.

'Oh, that's easy,' replied Antonia. 'The Montecutes have got one that takes tourists around their park to see the attractions, so our cousins James and Sebastian are going to "borrow" it for the day.'

'That's amazing!' giggled Penny.

'It's going to be a hoot,' said Antonia.

'Our ghost-train ride will be spine-chilling!' said Arabella.

'We are setting up arenas at the front of the house on the lawns,' said Antonia, 'and we're hoping you'd be able to join us for some of the events, Penny.'

Penny said she would try but would have to be with her own human family a good deal of the time. She was looking forward to the working hunter Class, because she thought she had a good chance of winning. Potty Smythe had asked her old friend Dame Gilly Jumpwell to judge the competition.

Later that morning, Penny took Sophie to the stable yard to meet the ponies. They were fascinated by her and wanted to hear about all the enchanted ponies that lived in the Underbelly of Equitopia. Of course Sophie remained invisible to the other humans on the stable yard, but everybody wondered why all the ponies galloped over to see Penny when she crossed their park. They had no idea there was a Centaureen walking by her side.

Matt was keen to show Shaab to Penny. He was a stunning white grey with a flowing silver mane and tail. He had huge dark eyes with white lashes. The beautiful horse rushed over to the stable door when he heard Matt approach.

Shaab was fascinated with Sophie as he had never seen a Centaureen. He stood snorting, with his ears pricked, as if frozen to the ground.

'He's seen something very strange,' said Matt, who of course could not see Sophie or understand pony language.

'It's OK, Shaab,' said Penny in Equalese. 'This is Fetlocks Hall – extraordinary things happen here but there is no need to be frightened. This is Princess Sophie of the Centaurs.'

'Good morning, oh Royal Highness,' said Shaab, immediately calming down and nuzzling Penny's ear.

'It was predicted that I should meet a Unicorn Princess here and that you would speak to me in my own language.'

'I know by your name that you are from the Royal family of the Four Winds,' said Penny. 'Matt is very lucky to have you as his friend.'

'Matt is very gifted,' said Shaab, 'but he has much to learn. One day he will show himself worthy to be a Knight of Equitopia. He will have charge of defending the reigning Princess in battle and will be greatly honoured by King Valentine Silverwings.'

Penny wondered how he knew this.

'I think Shaab has the fortune-telling power of the Four Winds,' whispered Sophie.

Penny thought this was a useful gift.

'He's incredible, Matt,' she said, stroking the horse's long silver forelock.

'Beautiful, isn't he?' said Henry as she walked past with some new feed buckets. 'How was the family, Penny?'

'Oh, fine really,' said Penny, 'just a quick visit for a birthday party.' She could not possibly tell Henry that it was her royal family of unicorns she had visited and the party she had gone to was Sophie's brother's crazy birthday stampede.

'Miss Manning-Smythe tells me you are all due for

a treat tomorrow,' continued Henry. 'We are taking the ponies down to the beach for a gallop along the sands and a picnic. I've told the others and they are all really looking forward to it.'

'Fantastic!' said Penny.

CHAPTER NINE

Thank You, Sea Horse

A shaft of bright morning sunlight burst in through the stained-glass window above the great hall at Fetlocks.

Mrs Honeybun had been busy in the kitchen since daybreak making sandwiches and scrumptious cakes for the picnic. She'd bottled home-made ginger beer and elderflower cordial to take with them. Sydney Sidewinder, the school janitor, was given the job of taking the picnic hampers over to the stable yard to be loaded into the school horseboxes.

'Mind you put them drinks in the lorry fridges,' she reminded him, 'and don't you scoff none of them almond slices now – they's for the children!'

Mrs Dogberry had already sent the janitor over with a pile of beach towels. Ben and Henry were up earlier than usual, loading tack into the wagons.

'The vet thinks this is a great idea,' Henry told Ben. 'He says seawater is excellent for the ponies' legs.'

The ponies had never been to the beach before or even seen the sea so Henry was hoping they would not be frightened by it. However, Patch had already told them Penny said that it was going to be great fun.

'I can't think why Potty Smythe has decided to do this at the last minute,' said Carlos, who would have been happier staying behind to practise for the polo match. 'After all, she's letting Merc and Morri stay at home to work on their display.'

The Veggipires were keeping what they were doing for their event under their hats as they wanted it to be a surprise for everyone.

Dom was delighted to be going to the beach and packed his surfboard and wetsuit into the lorry. He'd already looked at the surf report for the area on the internet and there were some big waves forecast.

Everybody had brought their swimsuits, even Potty Smythe, who had not worn one for a good many years. It was black with a funny little skirt attached, and stretchy, which was a great help!

Pip and Sam sang 'Oh we do like to be beside the seaside' as they put travel boots and tail guards on the ponies.

Sophie was waiting in the yard for Penny. She was going to travel, invisibly, with them in the tack part of the lorry, between the horses and the living area.

It was a perfect day for the beach. The sun shone in a cloudless blue sky as the two lorries driven by Henry and Ben made their way down the drive and out of the school gates towards the coast road. It only took three quarters of an hour to reach their destination. They pulled into the car park and set down the ramps to unload the ponies.

'No saddles,' said Potty Smythe. 'Seawater is bad for leather.'

It was decided to go for a gallop along the beach and a paddle in the sea before lunch so everyone slipped into their swimsuits and vaulted up on to their ponies' backs. Potty Smythe was keeping an eye out for Mr and Mrs Horsington-Charmers' arrival.

She hoped the Kelpies would keep their promise and that Pip's parents would somehow turn up.

Dom and Sir Fin were used to the sea so Dom offered to give everyone a lead. The children and ponies trotted over the dunes towards the sparkling blue ocean. Soon they were all cantering along the five miles of beach and really enjoying themselves.

'Come on, let's have a race,' said Sam, ready to let Landsman go.

'You're on!' shouted Matt, no stranger to sand racing with his magnificent Arab horse. Shaab leapt forward and was way ahead of the others in seconds. He flew like the wind and left them far behind.

'That's incredible!' said Carlos. 'I *want* one of those! He's going to be great on our polo team!'

Penny and Patch were having fun with Sophie galloping along by their side.

'I wonder when the Kelpies are going to show up with Pip's parents,' said Penny. 'Banjax promised they'd meet us with them as soon as we brought Pip to a beach.'

Sophie said she did not trust Kelpies and they probably would not turn up, but Penny was counting on it.

After their long gallop they decided to take the ponies for a paddle. Dom told everyone to follow him as he walked Sir Fin into the sea. At first the other ponies were a little apprehensive of the waves. Waggit had overcome his fear of jumping into water on cross-country courses but this was different.

Suddenly a big wave came towards him and he tried to jump it. Pip slipped off with a splash and landed up to her waist in the water.

There was a sudden swirl and Penny and Sophie saw a green pony head with a mane of seaweed pop out of the waves.

'Be careful, Penny, it's a Kelpie!' shouted Sophie in Equalese.

But before she and Penny could do anything Pip had jumped on to its back and it was swimming out to sea with her!

Penny realised that the Kelpie must have shape-shifted into something Pip recognised.

'Come back, Pip,' she yelled. 'It's not real!'

But her friend could not hear her.

None of the other children except Penny and Sophie could see the Kelpie swimming away with Pip. To them she had simply disappeared!

Dom threw Sir Fin's reins to Carlos and plunged into the water to look for her. He was a strong swimmer but could not find Pip anywhere. Everyone was very worried. Sophie pulled out her bow and arrows and took aim but did not loose her arrow because she was frightened she might hit Pip instead of the Kelpie.

Penny galloped Patch into the deep water after them.

'I can't swim!' said the little pony, now struggling out of his depth.

'But you can fly,' said Penny.

'I'm scared,' cried Patch. 'There are too many waves and I won't be able to take off.'

'You are the bravest pony in the world,' said Penny, stroking his soaking wet brown and white neck. 'Just pretend you are a seaplane . . . now, LET'S FLY!'

Patch paddled hard with his legs. The water seemed to be holding him down but with one big jump he freed himself from it and soared into the sky.

To everyone else except Sophie, it just looked as if Penny and Patch had disappeared beneath the waves as well.

'Come on,' said Dom, vaulting on to his pony. 'We have to get back to the lorries like lightning and tell Potty Smythe to call the coastguard. This is really urgent!'

It was five miles back to the wagons and the ponies were tired after their long gallop.

'I'll go,' said Matt. 'Shaab can do it. You lot stay here and mark the spot where they were last seen.'

With that he turned his horse and sped away over the sand, leaving his friends standing in the surf.

Penny steered Patch towards the Kelpie, who, with Pip stuck to his back, was swimming hard in the deep blue water below them.

Pip had no idea what was really happening. The Kelpie had shape-shifted and appeared to her as her parents and their dinghy, *Windflower*! The Kelpie had hypnotised her into thinking they were all going sailing together as one happy family as they used to do when on holiday in Cornwall. She did not know that she was riding on a dangerous creature whose intention was to lure her into the sea, plunge below the waves and drown her!

Penny had to think quickly.

'Right, Patch,' she said. 'As soon as it looks as if the Kelpie is going to dive, I want you to zoom down towards him. Then I'll jump off and grab his tail. I will give you enough power to fly on your own because you're going to have to whizz up very quickly so you don't plunge head first into the sea. The power will last long enough for you to fly back to the others.'

'But what about you?' cried Patch. 'You will go down with Pip and be drowned!'

'No, I won't,' replied Penny. 'Don't forget, I AM a Unicorn Princess. Quick, there he goes!'

The little pony did as he was told and skydived down towards the water until he was on top of the Kelpie's wake. Penny slid off Patch into the sea and grabbed the creature's tail, taking a gulp of air as they plunged beneath the waves. Patch soared up and away to safety, then headed for the shore.

Pip stayed stuck to the Kelpie's back until it reached the sea bottom, where it bucked her off. Penny let go of its tail and grabbed her friend. It gave her a wild angry stare as it shot past her like a torpedo, making for the surface. It was short of air because it had been made to swim harder owing to the extra weight of Penny holding on to its tail. Penny had to act quickly in case it came back to finish them both off.

Pip felt very limp and Penny was running out of air in the dark water. She looked up at the sunlight coming from above and with one arm around Pip's waist started to swim towards it.

Then a really scary thing happened. Penny's foot got stuck in something that prevented her from swimming. She thrashed around in the water as a piece of trawler netting wrapped itself around her legs!

Penny thought she was going to drown with Pip but suddenly there was a swish in the water and a beautiful white creature which seemed to be half horse and half sea serpent glided out of the gloom towards her. He quickly bit through the net, setting her free to climb on to his back. She was still holding on to Pip, who was very weak now. Another sea horse appeared and took hold of the cross straps of Pip's swimsuit with its teeth. Together they hauled her friend's limp body up in front of Penny.

In a flash they swam towards the light to reach the surface with its clean, cold, welcoming air. Penny spluttered, gasped and filled her lungs with it. All around her, bobbing in the waves, were hundreds of lovely white sea horses.

Pip was blue with the cold and appeared lifeless in her arms.

'Pip!' she cried. 'Wake up . . . oh, please wake up!' But her friend did not answer.

One of the sea horses swam up and put his nostrils close to Pip's open mouth. He breathed a puff of blue sparkling air into it so that she coughed and sputtered up a lungful of seawater.

'Thank you, sea horse,' breathed Penny with tears in her eyes.

'My pleasure, Princess Penny,' he replied. 'King Valentine sent us when he saw you were in danger from his crystal cloud.'

'Where are we?' murmured Pip.

'Just hold on to me,' said Penny. 'You are in safe hands.'

The sea horses turned and swam like a pod of dolphins towards the beach. The waves were enormous now. Dom had been right. It was brilliant for surfing! Between the crashing foam Penny could see the other children and ponies waiting on the shore. The great white horses surfed down the waves with Penny and Pip clinging to the leader. As the last wave broke the horses disappeared completely, leaving the girls to wade out of the water.

'There they are! She's got her!' shouted Dom, splashing towards them. He grabbed Pip and hoisted her up on to Waggit.

'Are you OK to ride?' he asked her.

Pip nodded and hung on to Waggit's mane.

Sam came forward on Landsman, leading Patch so that Dom could help Penny on to her pony before vaulting on to Sir Fin.

'You did it!' said Patch as they galloped back up the beach.

'Thanks to you!' said Penny, hugging him around his neck.

'Not a bad bit of bodysurfing, Pony Pen!' grinned Dom, who had seen nothing of the white sea horses but only Penny sliding over the waves with Pip in tow.

'You'd make a good lifeguard!' laughed Sam.

'We thought you were both goners for a moment,' said Carlos, 'especially when Patch came back without you, Penny. Then seconds later there you both were, like magic!'

They continued up the beach and came to a halt.

'Are you OK, Pip?' said Penny.

'Yes, I think so,' she said, none the worse for her undersea adventure thanks to the magical breath of the sea horse. 'I must have blacked out or something when I fell off Waggit because I had this weird dream that I was sailing with Mummy and Daddy. Then the next thing I knew you had hold of me and we were swimming in big waves. Penny, you saved my life!'

Everyone was congratulating Penny when they heard a shout behind them. Matt and Shaab came galloping down a dune from the direction of the road.

'Thank goodness you're safe!' he said. 'As soon as I told the grown-ups we stuffed Shaab in one of the lorries and drove up here as fast as we could. Oh, here they come.'

He pointed towards Potty Smythe, Ben and Henry, running towards them across the dunes. Suddenly two other grown-ups appeared on the top of a nearby sand dune and made their way towards the group of children.

'Who are they?' said Matt.

Pip's eyes nearly popped out. She could not really believe what she was seeing. For a moment she could not move.

'IT'S MUMMY AND DADDY!' she cried.

'Pip, darling!' shouted her mother.

Pip cantered up to them on Waggit and jumped off into their arms.

Penny and Sophie smiled secretly at each other.

Paul and Moggy Horsington-Charmers threw their arms around their daughter. All three of them entwined in a big family hug.

'Oh, Mummy,' said Pip between tears of joy, 'I thought I'd never see you and Daddy again!'

Potty Smythe, Ben and Henry joined the others, followed by Pip, Waggit and her parents. Paul and Moggy introduced themselves.

'This is all quite enchanting!' said Potty Smythe. 'It's wonderful to meet you at last.'

'It's magic,' said Pip's dad, 'in every sense of the word, because we aren't sure how we actually got here!'

Henry and Ben looked puzzled. The other children stared at each other in amazement. Penny came over and gave Pip a hug.

'You two girls gave us a nasty scare,' said Potty Smythe, who had sent an S.O.S. to the coastguard.

Their yellow helicopter was hovering over the sea, so she called them again on her mobile phone to say everything was all right and the children were safe and well.

'You missed a real sea rescue,' said Carlos.

'Pip disappeared under the waves and Penny fished her out!' added Sam.

'Penny bodysurfed in, towing her!' added Dom.

Everyone thought Penny had been so brave. Mr and Mrs Horsington-Charmers could not thank her enough. They all crowded round and gave her a good Fetlocks Hall Flyers view holla.

'I'm starving,' Penny said, laughing. 'Didn't we come here for a picnic or something?'

Henry and Ben sorted out the ponies while Potty Smythe unpacked the hampers. The children dried themselves with towels and everyone, except Sophie, who still had some berrymunders left, tucked into Mrs Honeybun's delicious packed lunch.

Dom could not leave without a ride on his surfboard so after lunch he gave them all a demonstration.

'Come on, Penny,' he called from the water as he sat astride his board. 'Come out here and have a go – you're a natural!'

'Not this time,' she called back. 'I've had enough of the sea for one day.'

CHAPTER TEN

Home to the Underbelly

On the way back to the school Penny asked Sophie to explain why the Kelpies had returned the lost parents at all.

'Ah, you see,' said her friend, 'it must have been their idea all along to get Pip. The Kelpie shape-shifted himself into the image of her parents and their dinghy to lure her on to his back, where she would stick fast so that he could dive down and drown her. Thanks to you, he did not get his way and could not return to finish you both off because you broke the Kelpie spell by saving Pip's life. Breaking the enchantment also set the parents free. They will know nothing about what happened to them because the Kelpies would have wiped it from their memory. They will simply think they lost their memory, which will explain why they disappeared without trace and for such a long time.'

In fact, that was exactly what happened, but her parents did get quite a shock when Pip told them they had been away for two years with no word!

'One minute we were pulling an injured zebra out of a swamp,' explained Pip's father to Potty Smythe, 'and the next moment we were here on the sand dunes running towards our daughter!'

Penny and Sophie looked at each other.

'Maybe there really are Zebra Kelpies of Zulupopo after all,' giggled Sophie.

It was getting dark when the lorries pulled into the stable yard at Fetlocks Hall. Sophie told Penny she thought she'd head off back to the Underbelly that night as Pip's parents had now been found and she was getting a bit homesick.

'Now I have slain a Minotorse,' she said, smiling, 'my life will be much happier with my herd.'

Penny told Sophie she'd miss her terribly but she understood. She was missing her own family and looking forward to seeing them at parents' day, which wasn't far off now. As it was a long way for Sophie to travel on hoof, Penny had the clever idea of flying her to Wiltshire with Patch. After all, she knew she could fly two ponies at the same time because she had once rescued Waggit from falling into a quarry while Equibatic on Patch.

Although Potty Smythe was sorry to see the Centaureen go, she was relieved Sophie had given up the idea of being a pupil at Fetlocks Hall as it was quite clear she was not cut out for it.

That night when everybody was asleep, Penny put Patch's bridle on and led him over to where her friend stood outside the Hall talking to the headmistress, with Hippolita and Rain by her side.

She vaulted up on to Sophie's back and slipped the school scarf round her friend's waist. Potty Smythe handed her Patch's reins and waved goodbye as the three of them took off in the moonlight.

Over the hills and woods they flew, looking down on the lights from the towns and cars beneath until they soared over the downs towards the Great White Horse carved in the chalk hillside.

Penny settled Sophie and Patch on the ground and slipped off her friend's back. Penny was not very good at goodbyes and felt she might cry. She fought back the tears as she and Sophie stood holding hands by the side of the horse's eye.

Suddenly the eye flipped up and a familiar shaft of light shot out. The two princesses grinned as one by one dozens of beautiful unicorns flew out of the entrance to Equitopia. The unicorns settled around them in a circle as a fanfare of trumpets sounded and King Valentine Silverwings himself joined them.

'Well done, you two!' he said.

'Thank goodness you were watching over me, Your Majesty!' said Princess Penny. 'You saved both Pip and me from drowning by sending the sea horses to rescue us.'

'It was quite an adventure!' agreed Sophie. 'But it's time for me to go home now.'

'And here is your escort!' said the King, pointing to the flight of unicorns, who all bowed down on one knee.

'But I can't fly without Penny,' said Sophie.

'Oh yes, you can, Princess Sophie of the Centaurs, because I will bestow upon you the power of Equibatics in return for your bravery and modesty. Princess Penny does not know what happened on the shore when that

Kelpie came out of the water. It was going to use its horrid tricks to select the other Fetlocks Hall children as prey. Princess Sophie galloped into the sea and grabbed it by its mane. She drew her sword and told it if the Kelpies ever tried anything like that again or ever came near any other children they'd have the Centaurs to deal with. The Kelpies are cowards really and will not risk a battle with Sophie's tribe, so all children are safe from them now.'

'Hurrah!' said Penny. 'You never said anything about that, Sophie!' she continued. 'You are so brave!'

'You were busy at the time,' said Sophie with a grin.

The King of the Unicorns moved his head with its beautiful golden horn in a circle. Sparkling stardust twinkled out of the horn and settled on the little Centaureen. Princess Sophie looked at her sides. To her delight she had grown two handsome wings!

'WOW!' she said. 'Thanks, Your Majesty!'

'You are the first one of your kind that can fly,' said King Valentine.

'Watch this, Penny!' said an excited Sophie, flapping her new wings and rising into the air. 'How do I look?'

'Pretty cool, I'd say,' said Penny with a smile.

'I'm jealous!' added Patch.

The flight of unicorns rose into the air and flew around Sophie.

'I'll see you two soon,' she called, waving goodbye as she sped down the shaft of light with her escort.

King Valentine rubbed his nose on Penny's cheek. 'I am so pleased with you, Princess Penny,' he said and vanished after them.

The eye slotted back into its place and Penny hopped on to Patch.

'Come on, boy,' she said. 'It's just you and me again now. *LET'S FLY!*'

And away they soared under the stars, back to Fetlocks Hall.

CHAPTER ELEVEN

A Wet Start

Time seemed to go very quickly once Sophie had returned home. Preparations for the two parents' days, visible and invisible, were going well. Invitations had been sent out and Potty Smythe had put advertisements in various newspapers to announce the live event, hoping prospective parents, looking for pony schools for their children, might come along.

Don Frederico Cavello, Carlos's father, was going

to come down to Dorset after the Royal International Horse Show and bring his puissance horse, Negra, for Carlos's high-jump display.

Matt was astounding everybody with his practice sessions on Shaab. He got the others to line up a row of watermelons stuck on bean poles, then he galloped his horse past them swinging his scimitar, a sort of curved sword, slicing the melons in half with one cut!

Mrs Honeybun, who was watching from the kitchen window, said he'd be very useful cutting up fruit for the trifles she was making for the parents' lunch.

Penny and Patch had their eye on the prize for the working hunter competition, so were frequently seen whizzing around the cross-country course at Fetlocks or practising over the show jumps, but Sam thought she could beat Penny on Landsman or her other pony, Hob.

Dom floated around the new outdoor ménage on Sir Fin, perfecting his dressage, and The Fetlocks Hall Flyers polo team and mounted-games team brushed up on their moves.

Pip had been given time off to spend with her parents as she had not seen them for so long. They'd gone back to the New Forest to set up their veterinary practice once more. Pip spent a few happy days with them there before returning to school to get Waggit ready for the show. She could not wait to see her mum and dad again on parents' day.

Henry bustled around the yard giving everybody orders and putting final details together for the parents' tour. The arenas were set up and Ben had built a testing course in the front park for the working hunters.

The teachers arranged some interesting projects in the classrooms. Miss Matisse, the Art teacher, had organised a lovely exhibition of equestrian art, paintings and sculpture by the students in a marquee on one of the lawns.

Meanwhile, the Fitznicelys were working on their archery, sword-fighting and side-saddle riding displays. Arabella and Antonia had decided to perform a pas de deux to music. Arabella had been downloading suitable music from the Internet on one of the school computers. She had chosen some dance music from an old movie called *Top Hat*.

Their cousins, Sebastian and James, had invented all sorts of scary things for their ghost-train ride. They'd even asked Count Blackdrax to appear on his terribly ugly horse.

'That'll be enough to scare anyone if it's anything like its portrait!' said Penny.

The morning of the parents' day could have been better. It was tipping down with rain, which was disappointing considering they had not had any for about a month!

Potty Smythe stood in the window of H.Q., staring out at the soggy parkland. She'd planned for the whole school, ponies, children and teachers, to line the drive and cheer the parents in as they arrived, but the weather had put paid to that. She made her way out on to the landing above the great hall to tell the pupils and staff that the drive reception was off.

As she appeared a huge cheer went up. Everybody was assembled below wearing raincoats and wellingtons and carrying umbrellas. Children waved hockey sticks and jumping whips in the air and the teachers unfolded a large banner they had made out of a long piece of plastic which read, *Welcome to Fetlocks Hall, an Unusual Pony School Where Extraordinary Things Happen!*

'You didn't think a little thing like water would put us off, did you, Miss?' said Penny, and they all laughed as they piled out to line the drive just before the first cars started to arrive.

First was Bunty Bevan, Penny's original riding

instructress and the person responsible for getting her into Fetlocks Hall. She had driven her old red Land Rover stuffed with terriers and Penny's family all the way from Milton Keynes.

Penny jumped up and down with excitement. Her sisters, Bella and Sarah, leaned out of the window and yelled, 'Hi, Pony Pen!' Oliver, her little brother, squealed with joy.

'Ollie ride ponies!' he said, wriggling in his childseat.

'Charlotte's on her way,' Mr Simms called out, pointing behind the car as they drove past.

A motorbike driven by Penny's older sister swung through the gates.

'Charlotte! You passed your test!' screamed Penny excitedly.

'Whoopee!' said Charlotte. 'I'll give you a ride later!'

Dom's parents arrived in their old hippy camper van with surfboards strapped to the roof. The Khareefs, Matt's parents, swished by in a chauffeur-driven Rolls-Royce. Merc and Morri's parents arrived in a carriage drawn by two black horses! Pip's turned up in a van with *New Forest Equine Veterinary Services* written on it.

Sam felt a bit left out. Her Auntie Sue was coming, but she didn't like horses at all because of what had happened to her sister and brother-in-law. Sam concentrated on memorising the working hunter course instead.

Back at the Hall Potty Smythe gave her old friend Bunty Bevan a hug,

'Oh good,' said the headmistress as a sleek blue sports car sloshed in through the gates. 'Here's Gilly – she's going to judge for us today!'

'How does she do it?' said Bunty Bevan as the glamorous Dame Gilly Jumpwell parked her smart car. 'She never seems to look any older than thirty and she's at least our age, Potty, old thing!'

'I heard that,' said Gilly as she climbed up the steps towards them. 'It's horses and the magical places they take you that keep you young.' The three old friends laughed and hurried inside out of the rain.

The school looked splendid. Mrs Dogberry, with old Mr Pennypot's help, had decorated it with impressive flower arrangements.

The dripping wet children, parents, teachers and other members of staff assembled in the great hall. Penny ran over to her family and her dad hoisted her up on to his shoulders. From here she could see all her friends with their own families including Ben with his parents, Willy and Kathleen Faloon, from Cork.

'How's our little princess?' said Willy, striding over

in a soaking wet raincoat and flat cap. He shook her dad's hand and said the Simms would be welcome in the Ballywater Valley should they ever come to Ireland.

Penny was having a great time introducing her family to her Fetlocks Hall friends. They were delighted Penny seemed so popular and incredibly proud of her when Mr and Mrs Horsington-Charmers told them how she had saved their daughter's life.

Sydney Sidewinder sounded the gong by Sir Walter's suit of armour to signal the start of the welcome speech.

'Ladies and gentlemen,' began the headmistress from the top of the stairs. 'It gives me great pleasure to see you all here today. On behalf of all our children, ponies and staff, I'd like to welcome you to Fetlocks Hall. We hope you all enjoy the show we have put on for you today in spite of the weather! As you can see from your programmes, the first event is a tour of the school and classrooms. We will start with the main house, so please follow me into our first port of call, the ballroom.'

Potty Smythe descended the stairs and strode across the hall to open the ballroom doors. To everyone else except Potty Smythe, Penny and the Fangley-Fitznicelys, the ballroom looked like a gymnasium, because that is what it was used for these days, but Penny's eyes lit up when she walked in to see the elegant room looking exactly as it used to in the eighteenth century. The chandeliers glittered, the long windows were hung with pink and lavender velvet curtains, The Headless Quartet were playing Mozart and it was full of the Fitznicelys' friends and family in full morning dress at their champagne reception.

Of course, she could not say anything when Arabella and Antonia bustled up with their cousins, James and Sebastian.

'Beats your do, doesn't it?' laughed the twins.

Penny smiled and nodded.

The parents continued on their tour of the class-rooms and then out into the stable yard to meet the ponies.

CHAPTER TWELVE

The Working Hunters

Penny took her family to see Patch as she tacked him up ready for the working hunter competition.

The rain was still pouring down when the competitors walked the course. Ben's Irish bank was huge. The ponies had to jump on to it, hop over a rail on the top and then slide down a steep drop on the other side.

There were fourteen riders entered. Gilly Jumpwell

and Bunty Bevan, who was stewarding for her, stood in the middle as the first competitor, Gig on her pony, Mouse, trotted into the ring. Unfortunately she was eliminated for having three refusals at the first jump. Gig was very disappointed in Mouse, who obviously did not like the slippery conditions at all.

The next three competitors did not make it up the bank so they were disqualified. Penny rode in on Patch, saluted to the judge and set off on her round. Patch loved jumping and neatly cantered around the course. He popped up the bank, nipped over the rail on the top and carefully slid down the slippery slope on the other side to cheers from the crowd for a nice clear round.

Waggit and Pip were next, but had the gate down, so got ten faults. Sam came in with Landsman and did a brilliant round with no faults at a real hunting pace.

Carlos also jumped round clear on Ned Kelly, Henry's former racehorse. Three other children and their ponies did nice rounds but Emily Gould knocked the rail down on top of the bank to get ten faults. The two Mayo boys went clear on their super ponies.

Sam came back in with her second pony, Hob, and did another great clear round. Now she had both ponies through to the next part of the competition in which they had to be ridden around the ring, without jumping, to show off their paces and manners. Sam had expected this but knew she could not ride both ponies in the ridden section, so she'd asked Matt to ride Hob for her.

All the ponies that had not been eliminated were invited back into the ring for the next phase of the competition. Patch went really well but Waggit looked even better, so Gilly Jumpwell pulled Pip in to stand at the top of the line in the winning position so far, with Penny and Patch in second. Landsman with Sam stood third and Hob, ridden by Matt, lay in fourth position. Ned had been a bit strong when the ponies had to gallop down the long side of the arena so Carlos was only called in fifth. The rest of the competitors lined up in order below him.

All the riders were then invited to do a short individual show in front of the judge. Waggit, with his pretty show-pony paces, did the best one. Patch tried hard but could not match it. Sam's two ponies went very well but Ned, now too excited after his gallop, could not stand still at the end of his display and Carlos knew he'd lose points for it.

The third phase of the competition involved removing the saddles and standing the ponies up in front of the judge for her to assess their good looks and suitability to be working hunters. Then they had to be walked and trotted past her so she could see how well they moved.

For each of the three sections of the class the judge awarded points which were added up at the end to find the winner. Pip knew she had not done so well in the jumping but hoped she had made up enough points in the ridden section to keep her place at the top of the line-up.

There was quite a tense moment as Gilly Jumpwell walked down the line of ponies, carefully giving each one a last look. She and Bunty Bevan consulted the score sheet under an umbrella in the pouring rain. The parents, also dripping wet, stood poised around the arena trying to guess the winner.

Gilly looked as though she had nearly made her decision. Bunty Bevan asked Pip to lead the others round the arena at a walk so that the judge could finally make up her mind and pick the winners in order.

The judge took a good look at Patch and Penny but then suddenly turned away and pointed at Sam on Landsman!

Sam gave Lannie a huge pat on the neck and walked into first place. Hob and Matt were chosen second. Penny's heart sank. She wanted to be at least third – but would Gilly choose her?

To her relief Bunty Bevan beckoned her to line up beside Matt in third place and her heart started beating again.

The Mayo boys came in fourth and fifth with Pip in sixth place. She was disappointed to have been put down from first but knew clear rounds count in this sort of competition. Her parents, however, were still very proud of her.

Gilly asked Bunty Bevan to bring over the basket of rosettes and a huge silver trophy given by Willy Faloon. She handed a big red rosette to Sam, who reached down and fastened it to Lannie's bridle below his left ear. She proudly posed with Gilly, holding the cup between them for the photographers. Gilly turned and patted Landsman.

'Cracking round, Sam,' she said, smiling. 'You won that for showing the best hunting pace. Your parents would have been proud of you. Hob went super but not quite so forward-going as this pony. Well done for being first and second.'

Sam grinned and thanked the judge.

Penny pinned on her third-place rosette and congratulated Sam and Matt.

Bunty Bevan asked Sam to lead the others round the ring in a lap of honour. The crowd cheered like mad.

'Come on,' yelled Sam to the other children following her. 'Let's go for the bank!'

The response was a shrill view holla from her friends, so she turned Landsman and cantered down the arena to jump the big obstacle and slide down the far side. The others followed her as she broke into a cracking gallop round the ring, splashing mud all over the following riders to the roar of the crowd.

CHAPTER THIRTEEN

Hooray for Fetlocks Hall

It was a very wet but delighted bunch of parents that sloshed their way back across the park and into the Hall for lunch. It was just as well they could not see the end of the sword-fighting display between Sir Walter and Sir Rupert that was going on at the same time. Sir Walter was clashing steel with his brother-in-law on the stairs when Sir Rupert tripped and fell backwards, tumbling down the flight and crashing into the gong, which made a loud 'boing' at exactly one o' clock.

'Oh, there's the dinner gong!' said Potty Smythe, who of course was the only one who saw the whole thing but had to reason away the unexpected noise.

Mrs Honeybun had prepared a wonderful cold buffet for the guests, but because everyone was so cold and wet she had quickly made a lovely cream of leek and potato soup with hot bread rolls to warm them up.

By two o'clock the rain had stopped but the ghost train had started. The Fitznicelys' guests were all queuing up for a good scary ride around the grounds as the parents made their way over to watch The Fetlocks Hall Flyers give their mounted-games display.

The children had decided on a coconut-shy race, where ponies carrying two riders would gallop down to a row of coconuts placed in holders. The pillion rider was to dismount and knock off a coconut with three balls previously placed on the ground. Once they had used up all the balls or knocked down a coconut they had to leapfrog back on to the ponies behind the front rider, then race to the finish. The first pony and riders past the finishing line would win the competition.

Penny, partnered by Pip, had slipped off Patch's back and chucked a ball at a coconut just as the ghost train whizzed past. She knocked off James de Parrott's head instead of the coconut, but luckily Arabella caught it and tossed it to her cousin, who screwed it back on. The ghostly passengers all applauded as they thought this was an intentional part of the show.

Penny reached for another ball, whacked the coconut, ran and leapfrogged on to Patch behind Pip, who galloped them back to the finishing line to win the race! Everyone cheered.

Nobody, dead or alive, was going to miss the polo match.

The polo ground was pretty slippery by now, but that was not going to stop Carlos, captain of the boys' team consisting of himself, Dom, Matt and Morri, from competing. Neither did it faze the girls' team, with Merc as captain, Sam, Pip and Penny.

There was only time for four chukkas but it was a hard-fought, fast and furious match. The girls only beat the boys by one goal this time instead of their usual wipeout. The crowd loved it, particularly Don

Frederico, who came striding across the ground afterwards to congratulate the girls, especially Merc, who rode every chukka side-saddle.

After the match the ghosts disappeared for their croquet match. Lady Sarah crocked her sister's ball so hard it sailed over the trees and hit the weather-vane on top of the stable-yard clock. It fell on to the yard, landing in a very surprised old Mr Pennypot's wheelbarrow, who happened to be passing at the time.

Lady Sarah was delighted with the result. Having dealt her sister's ball a fatal blow she went on to win the match by hitting the stump.

'Croquet, I believe,' she said, smiling.

Meanwhile Dom floated into the ménage on Sir Fin and wowed the crowd with a wonderful freestyle dressage test. Afterwards Carlos rode into the ring looking super-fit and confident on Negra to give his puissance display.

Henry and Peter Fixcannon were in charge of increasing the height of the single pole Negra was going to jump. She had already won her class at the Royal International Horse Show earlier that week, setting a record height, but Carlos was hoping he could better it.

Negra easily flew over the first height. After each

successful attempt Henry and Peter raised the pole until it was higher than she had ever jumped before. Negra took off just in the right place to clear the fence and set a new world record for jumping a single pole!

Carlos punched the air as he rode round the ring. The crowd stood up and applauded. Don Frederico went crazy. Everyone crowded around Carlos and the little black mare, patting her and telling her what a clever girl she was.

The children helped prepare the arena for the next event, Matt's display of Arabian horsemanship.

He galloped into the ring on his stunning horse dressed in the flowing robes of a Bedouin warrior to the delight of the audience. He swung his scimitar high over his head and then leaned right over Shaab's side at full gallop. Slipping his stirrups, he kicked off the ground and spun himself back into the saddle still holding the sword. The crowd went wild. It really was a great show. Then Matt galloped down the row of watermelons and sliced them to bits.

He brought his horse to a halt and dismounted. Shaab stood still as his rider walked a short distance away from him. Matt turned, raised an arm and the horse reared up and walked on his hind legs towards the boy. Matt knelt down and Shaab copied him. He rolled on his side and the horse did the same, ending up with his head in Matt's lap.

Mr and Mrs Khareef were so proud of their son. The audience rose to their feet and cheered as Matt climbed on to Shaab's back while he lay on the ground. At his command the horse stood up, carrying his rider. He reared up on his hind legs, then bowed down on one knee to the crowd.

Matt raised both hands into the air as he galloped the lovely animal out of the arena. The rest of The Flyers ran over to congratulate him and Shaab.

'Crumbs,' said Penny. 'That really was awesome!'

'Thanks,' said Matt, as he stroked his horse's white neck. 'Shaab deserves all the praise. He is a prince among horses.'

Everybody was looking forward to the next thing on the programme.

Merc and Morri had been keeping their display a secret because they wanted it to be a big surprise finale to the show. They were going to act out a creepy theme to music on horseback.

Everyone sat in silence waiting for the start. Even the ghosts did not want to miss out on it, so they brought their tea things over to the arena to watch.

Uncle Faustus and Countess Mortia-Antoinette, Merc and Morri's parents, were busy setting up a music system with big speakers. Uncle Faustus was also carrying a black box with air holes in it.

The one-eyed hunchback, who worked for the Fangley-Fitznicelys, helped Uncle Faustus to haul a wooden coffin into the centre of the arena.

Merc, dressed in a black cloak, riding side-saddle on her pony, Nightsafe and leading her brother's pony, Moonwalk, waited at the entrance. Both ponies were also wearing matching black hoods and rugs.

Merc gave her father the signal to start the music, which sounded like a creaky door. Then she slowly rode into the ring in time to the sound of heavy footsteps. As the music broke into a spooky pop song she threw her cloak to the ground. Underneath she was dressed as the Bride of Frankenstein!

The crowd hooted with laughter and applauded loudly.

She and Morri had spent ages studying the skeleton of the horse from one of Peter Fixcannon's books on anatomy so that they could chalk the relevant bones all over their black ponies. When Merc pulled their rugs off and galloped the 'skeleton' ponies around the ring in time to the crazy music, the effect was astonishing! She aimed Nightsafe and Moonwalk towards the coffin and jumped it just as the music gave a ghostly laugh.

The coffin lid sprang open and out climbed Morri dressed as Count Dracula!

Merc trotted back to him with both ponies and Morri vaulted on to Moonwalk's back. Then the two of them rode around the arena to another wacky song, producing plastic snakes, false severed hands and other funny spooky things out of their costumes to toss at the crowd. Gilly Jumpwell shrieked as a large rubber spider landed in her lap.

At the end of the performance Uncle Faustus opened the black box and released his pet bats. They wheeled around Merc and Morri as they took their final bow, before heading off home to the Dower House.

The ghostly spectators thought this was the best show yet. Count Blackdrax laughed so hard his glass eye popped out and disappeared down the bodice of Lady Fitznicely's dress. Wincing, she bravely fished it out and handed it back to him.

All the Fetlocks children assembled in the arena and took a bow. They called for Potty Smythe to join them, but she declined until Gilly and Bunty Bevan gave her a push. She held the children's hands in the middle of the line for their second bow. The parents went wild.

'Hip hip hooray for Fetlocks Hall,' shouted Mr Horsington-Charmers.

Everyone joined in.

The show was over and the guests made their way back to the Hall for the farewell tea. They could not stop talking about their wonderful day. They thanked Potty Smythe for everything and said the great thing about the show was the way it had brought everybody's families together in the best way possible.

'It was all Penny's idea really,' said the headmistress.

It was time to go home. The parents said goodbye and left with happy memories. All were delighted they had made the decision to send their children to such a fantastic school. Potty Smythe was delighted, too, that several new parents had approached her and asked for a prospectus.

Penny was sad to see her family leave, but she would be seeing them all again soon in the holidays.

As dusk was falling she walked over to the stable yard to say goodnight to Patch and think about Sophie. She wondered how she was getting on with her own family back in the Underbelly. To her amazement she found all the stable doors open and the ponies gone! Penny thought she must find Henry and tell her what had happened, but just then she caught the faint sound of some awful but familiar music coming from the home paddock.

A smile broke over her face as she ran through the open gate to a stretch of green grass on the other side of the great oak trees.

To anyone else it would have looked as if the ponies had got loose and were having a great time careering around the field, but among them Penny could see dozens of Centaurs stampeding up and down to the music of their band, who were making their usual din!

Sophie galloped towards her out of the mass of horses.

'Come on, Penny,' she said. 'Everyone's here. I brought them over from Equitopia for an end-of-parents'-day party. They're teaching the ponies line dancing! You didn't think we'd miss out on the fun, did you?'

Penny laughed and hopped up on to Sophie's back.

'The fun never stops at Fetlocks Hall!' she said.

The two princesses looked up at the night clouds, watching as they slowly changed shape to form a flight of unicorns. As King Valentine Silverwings led them across the star-studded sky he waved to the two friends below. Penny and Sophie waved back before galloping away in a fit of giggles to join the pony party.

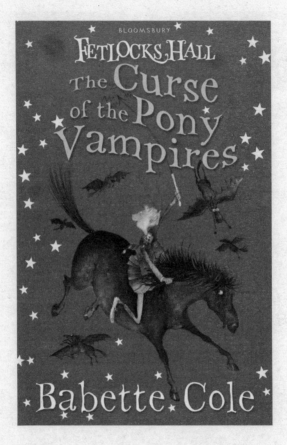